PORTRAIT OF A WIDE SEAS ISLANDER

VICTORIA GODDARD

1

Tovo spent his ninetieth year walking the Ring.

He started, as the old tradition had it, where he was when the idea came to him: the Mdang family house in Gorjo City, which his older sister had built when she decided to move with her new husband to the city and raise her family there.

It had been a large family by any standard, sixteen children by the time they had decided they were done. His sister had said they had sixteen because they had promised the gods to *extend their garden* as thanks for saving Kivor's life when he was caught in a hurricane at sea, but Tovo had always thought it was just because she had been told by an Astandalan physician that she did not have the right sort of hips for child-bearing.

The Mdangs had always had that contrary streak running through them.

Tovo was no different, really. He took his old vaha, the outrigger canoe that had served him well for well over seventy years now, and sailed off along the old, familiar ke'ea.

East first and then west, always the pattern for an Islander.

Instead of heading across the middle of the Bay of the Waters as he would if he were going straight home to his own island, he turned east and sailed the complicated currents between Gorjo City and the Gate of the Sea.

The channel out was marked by tall coral pillars, pale white with guano from the cormorants who perched on them. The coral looked like natural formations along the edges of the winding deepwater channels.

Shark roads, the city folk called them.

Roads was the Shaian translation for *ke'ea*. Tovo wasn't sure if it held all the weight *ke'ea* did. A ke'ea was the way you were guided by the stars in the night, the way from one island to the next when the next was far, far out of sight. You sang a chant of stars, from your island to wherever you were going, anchoring you into the greater shape of the Wide Seas, the greater pattern of the *Lays*.

A road, well, what was a road to a seafaring people? The current of other men's travels, Tovo guessed.

Tovo held his boat there in the middle of a rocking wave, just where several currents met and held back the tide. He handled the vaha easily, knowing these waters with the whole of his body. The air was salt and thick with guano. Seabirds were crying as they wheeled over the heights on either side of the Gate of the Sea.

He looked out, east, at the sun just rising. The spray glittered, as brilliant as sparks from a new fire, cast up by the waves breaking over the coral in a constant rumble and thunder. The boat quivered under his hand, the sail taut in the wind, the outrigger steady, the rudder firm.

The sun, the cool morning air, the seabirds, the ke'ea of the Sun. He had followed it once.

This morning he took a breath, spat over the edge of the canoe as an offering to those who held that channel open, and made the small constellation of movements that caused the boat to leap eagerly to the south and west, away from the Gate of the Sea and back into the embrace of the Ring.

There were a dozen uninhabited islands between the Gate of the Sea and the first of the Pirimiris. The most significant of these, and arguably not entirely uninhabited, was Pau'lo'en'lai, or Pau'en'lo'ai, or any of a number of related names. Under any name, the Isle of the Dead.

Tovo was not a superstitious man, but you did not have to be ninety to think about why such a journey, such a time to be Walking the Islands, would begin with the Gate of the Sea and continue on with the Isle of the Dead.

He drew his canoe up on the beach, tethering it to the stone post set there. He considered the supplies he had laid in for the first part of the circuit, and eventually selected his favourite obsidian knife. He considered the blade, the grey-black stone, somehow waxy looking, translucent if he held it up to the sun. The hilt, clay and plant fibre wound about the haft. The clay had been red to begin with, the same kind the people of Viluoa used to make cooking pots, but over the years the oils of his hand had darkened it to a definite brown, polished with use.

Pau'lo'en'lai was a high island, volcanic like most of those in this part of the Ring: the stone was black basalt and the rough kind of lava they called ai-ai. The beach was a narrow inlet of white sand leading up to the grassy headland between the foreshore and the jungle cladding the steep inland heights.

At the head of the beach was a tall stone ngali staff. Tovo walked up to it, examining the carved stone. It was maybe twenty feet high, and eight across. Twelve bands spiralled around a hollow centre from a stone pedestal to a crown of broad-petalled tui flowers. Tui flowers for the trees that

Islanders had always planted to mark their dwelling-places. Twelve spiralling bands for each of the twelve great lineages, the ships that had borne the first wayfinders to the Vangavaye-ve.

He found the band that was decorated with the Mdang family patterns, curved lines in a not-quite-regular pattern.

The Mdangs Held the Fire, and the fire was both always the same and always different.

Always that streak of the contrary in them, that moment between strike and spark where the world held its breath to see what flame would catch.

Most often Tovo lit a flame with a hibiscus-wood tinder-bed and a length of palm, or a bow drill: once you knew what you were doing, it was quick, almost easy. He had shown hundreds of people, old and young, how to do the same.

Tovo knew other ways to light a fire, of course, some modern and some very, very old. He could light a fire with one of the glass lenses the Astandalans had brought with them, and with their magic charms and their metal strikers.

There was a kind of stone that could make sparks. Or rather two—Tovo had a pair of them, at home on Loaloa. One, the tovo for which he had been named, was very common along the Ring, found on practically every beach. The other, which the Mdangs called tanaea—a word that also meant hearth, and the fire that goes in the hearth—had always been brought in from the other side of the world, even years and years ago before the coming of the Empire.

There was one source for the tanaea, one island known to the ancestors. It was far away in the west and north of the Wide Seas. It was mentioned in the *Lays* as one of the ancient secrets of the ancestors, long since lost.

Tovo knew the ke'ea for reaching it was deliberately incomplete.

The secret knowledge of the *Lays* held by the Mdangs told

how in the long ago the one who would be tana-tai, the one who sought to hold the fire for the next generation, would undertake a solitary voyage to find that island and retrieve one of the sacred fire-starting stones.

They would build a new fire with a spark struck from it, one stone from their own island, one stone from the other side of the world, to show their community that they knew both old and new, far and near, the ways of the sea and the needs of the hearth.

The other lore-keepers laughed sometimes at the small store of practical knowledge held by the tanà: what one needed to know in order to build a fire was hardly the same as being able to name every star in the sky, or every wind of the year, or how to make every kind of rope and twine and cloth anyone needed.

The tanà had another role, whose study was lifelong; and no one thought that holding the fire of the heart of the community was a task without skill or honour.

Tovo had gone looking for the island where the tanaea were to be found when he was a young man. He had already been acclaimed as tanà, given the efetana of fire coral by his great-uncle, and he had thought, rightly in the end, that he might become tana-tai. No one else had gone since.

Pau'lo'en'lai was a quiet place. The wind was still here, in the space around the ngali staff stele. The seabirds' cries seemed a long way away. The grass rippled in a wind he could not feel. The jungle in the distance was green and lush, full of birds that had barely seen human beings. Only those who were ready to join the Ancestors crossed the boundary marked by the stele; even those who were called to tend the dead stayed in the cleared area between beach and jungle.

The twelve stone houses of the dead stood with their backs to him, their faces to the mountain. Each of the primary lineages, the great ships that had brought the first families to the Vangavaye-ve, had their own house. Thousands of years of the bones of the Ancestors rested here, on this one island, given to the jungle. The lore-keepers of each lineage were those laid in the stone houses.

Tovo laid the obsidian knife on the offering-stone and spoke a prayer to the dead.

One day he would pass the boundary marked by the stele and prepare himself to join the Ancestors.

He was ninety, after all, and he could feel himself slowing down. This would likely be the last journey he took in his own canoe, certainly the last one by himself.

One day he would fall asleep at the edge of that unknown jungle and not wake up. One day his flesh would be stripped by the birds and insects of the island. One day his bones would be collected by those who served the dead and brought to lie in the stone house far to the right, last named in the *Lays*, the stone ship of Ouvaye-ve. One day he would be one of the Ancestors named in the prayers.

But not today.

He left the Isle of the Dead and followed the channels through the reefs, south and west in a great arc.

There were places on each of the named islands of the Ring where someone could bring a small vaha up to the land. You could not beach a canoe on each of them, of course— some were sheer pinnacles, where the seabirds peered down at him with wild, curious eyes. Yet even for those you could come close enough to touch.

No one lived on these islands, this far east. They were too close to the Gate of the Sea and the Island of the Dead. They were not exactly sacred, or not any more so than the rest of the islands, but there was a certain sense of trespass that many felt.

And of course it would be hard living here, with the surging tides and currents through the maze of reefs and pinnacles: there were few trees, few lagoons, few protected harbours, nowhere really to build a village that would not find itself stripped by the southeast tradewinds.

Tovo touched each island, naming them. Pauo and Paua; the chain of fifteen small islets called the Eastern Efela; Tepekarua where the shell-divers came for the purple-and-green warokainë shells; Tepekanui where there was a single, ancient ti palm, leaning far aslant and yet never quite falling.

Ti were sacred: they marked land, and held spirits, and were useful in all sorts of ritual, ceremonial, and practical activities. Elsewhere in the Ring people had selected ones with red leaves, or green, and there were many, many stories held by the Poyë lore-holders and old aunties alike about them.

Tepekanui sloped up towards the outside of the Ring, black stone rising up out of the soft white coral sand until the skyline of the island looked like a giant's teeth. Tovo beached his vaha and made his way up to the palm.

The ti was still leaning out at its mad angle. It had fallen down and then twisted up, so the trunk curved like a cupped hand holding a tufted bouquet of leaves. These were mottled green and gold, strikingly beautiful. Tovo had sometimes wondered why none of the Poyë or anyone else who liked gardening had come to take a cutting, but then again, ti trees *were* sacred, and to find one like this, solitary, contorted, old— and yet so beautiful—well, he was probably not the only one who had encountered the gods here.

Tovo had come here first when he was a mere stripling, sent by his own great-uncle to visit the tree and collect a kind of barnacle that clung to the rocks inside a cave below the ti palm.

The sea-cave was accessible only at a very low tide, when the ocean receded just enough that a daring person might be able to climb down the cliff and safely pass through the low tunnel leading to the cavern. The barnacles were to be found nowhere else, and Tovo had always wondered just who had discovered them.

A Walea youth studying to Hold the Eefela, looking to find a new shell to add to their store of knowledge? A Varga hunter, following the lure of danger and adventure? Someone fleeing a crime, or fleeing a criminal? Someone led by a spirit in the ti palm, a dream or a vision or a god?

Tovo touched his efela ko, fingers lingering on the two beads that were a deep, lustrous blue, the colour of the sky after sunset, with a shimmer like a birthing star.

His great-uncle had given him a riddle: Tovo had had to know the *Lays* well enough to determine which island he needed; he had needed to examine every inch of Tepekanui to find a shell he did not know; and he had needed to ask for assistance from the Walea lore-holder to learn how to turn the barnacles into the blue beads.

There had been no challenge for him in diving for the golden pearls. Even searching out the flame pearls at the edge of the deep ocean was something joyous and bright, a challenge to his strength and his knowledge and his skill.

But the barnacles, oh, they had been hard.

He had come back often to this place, to meet himself again and again, and thus, once or twice had he also met the god of mysteries here.

On this occasion he sat at the foot of the ti palm and looked at the waters foaming about the rocks far below.

The ti was on the eastern side of the island, looking out over the Wide Seas. Far, far away in that direction (and a little north) was where Kip lived.

Kip was his great-nephew and student of the lore, the one he had always intended and expected to follow him as tana-tai.

He had not sent Kip for the barnacles. Kip had found challenge enough in the pearls.

Kip who had hated pearl-hunting on the first dive, which Tovo had thought would be an easy entry into the study.

Kip who had refused to let his hatred and his fear stop him.

Kip who had sat at his feet and refused ever to give up.

Oh, Kip was a long way away, and had been gone a long time.

Tovo walked the Ring that year: he touched every named island and islet, walked upon each inhabited island and those which bore special memories for him.

This might be his last time Walking the Ring, his last time sailing the Ring on his own, in his old vaha. He could only hold the hope, one more ember in his fire-pot, that Kip would come with him next time, would be at his elbow, would be the one speaking truth, seeing clearly, holding the fire in his hands.

Tovo visited the people in villages who rarely had strangers come to their islands. He drank kava and coffee and coconut water and fruit juices and palm wine, ate what they offered him—fish and taro, octopus and chicken, breadfruit and tree fern and all the rest of the traditional foods.

There had never been many tanà around the Ring. For all the size of the Mdang family in recent generations, their traditional knowledge was a heavier burden than most of the lore keepers held. There were a dozen or more amongst the Kindraa who Knew the Wind and were great navigators, or Walea who Held the Efela, or Nevans who Tied the Sails and knew all the secrets for making the different kinds of ropes and twine and fabric a community might need.

There were three people who Held the Fire.

Tovo was the most senior, and the one to whom everyone came for serious problems around the Ring. His nephew Lazo in Gorjo City was always there with a listening ear and a helpful word for any of the problems the people in the city brought to him. And there was Kip.

Oh, there were chiefs and headmen, there were informal leaders and village Speakers, there were shamans and sacred fools, there were wise women and powerful matriarchs. All the people who guided their communities, who led their people—their families, their villages, their islands—who made the decisions that needed to be made to survive and thrive.

The tanà was not the chief or the paramount chief. Lazo was a barber; Tovo had been a pearl diver; Kip was ... whatever he was. They did not live in the big houses, were not the big men. No one pointed them out when visitors came.

They Held the Fire. They knew every Lay: not simply the public *Lays*, in Shaian and in language, but the full cycle that was sung over the twelve days of the Singing of the Waters.

Others knew the *Lays*, of course. It was part of the knowledge held by each of the lore-holders, their responsibility to ensure that the histories and legends and collective knowledge of their people was not lost. Each of the lore-holders held also the extra knowledge relating to their family's specialization.

The Mdangs knew how to build a fire and tend it.

More: the tanà knew how to build the fire of community and tend it.

They shared their gifts freely, holding that the greatest gift they could give their people, the greatest knowledge they held, was to give the coal that could light another fire.

Tovo had never turned anyone away, Mdang or not, who came to him to ask how to light a fire.

There had been dozens over the years who had sat at his feet, his and Lazo's too.

There were a dozen, perhaps, who had successfully

finished the first year of their apprenticeship, had made the efela ko by facing their fears and their weaknesses; learned the cycle of the *Lays*, perhaps even the first and easiest steps of the fire dance.

There were half a dozen who had gone on to hold the fire in their islands, villages, families. They had begun to take the *Lays* and reflect them back to the Islanders, teach them what the lore meant now.

There was one who had learned all Tovo could teach, and then sailed off, because someone always left.

Tovo still waited for his sail to come back over the horizon.

Tovo walked the Ring that year.

He knew people in most villages, every island. He had walked the Ring many times before, listening and looking, asking questions as necessary, learning the heart of the people, reflecting them back to themselves.

The tanà held the heart of the Islands, it was said.

They had the fire in their hands, and they held it out to those who needed it, and those who did not know they needed it.

He lit fire after fire, showing children and shy youths and shyer adults any of half a dozen ways to do so. He ate the food he was given, talked over the affairs of the Outer Ring islands with the elders in each community.

The elders of the Outer Ring knew the old traditions. They knew why Lazo was not accompanying him, for Lazo was the tanà but had never been the one to be called tana-tai.

Lazo had never sailed off to bring back a tanaea, a striking rock from the island on the other side of the world, with which he might light a new tanaea, a new hearth-fire.

There were a hundred good reasons why he hadn't, but

the fact remained that the reasons did not matter. He who would be tana-tai sailed across the Wide Seas in a boat of his own building to find a striking rock on the other side of the world. That was what he *was*. Lazo had not, and so he could be a most excellent tanà, but was not tana-tai.

The elders of the Outer Ring knew why Lazo did not sail with him, but they knew as well as Tovo did that there should have been a younger man to stand at his elbow.

Some of them merely looked meaningfully at the empty space beside him. Others asked.

"And where is the one who comes after you?" Kuaso of Iruzayë asked him.

"Someone always leaves," Tovo replied evenly. "He will come back when it is time."

Iruzayë was far to the west of the Ring, one of the Tirigilis. It was famous in the *Lays* for being the home of Elonoa'a, last of the Paramount Chiefs. Elonoa'a had discovered the Isolates, and for that alone he would have been named in the *Lays*, but he had also been the one who had brought the Islands into alliance with the Empire of Astandalas.

Elonoa'a had been famous for leaving.

More: for leaving in the company of an Emperor of Astandalas.

Kuaso grunted. He and Tovo had been lovers for a time, when they were both young and hot-blooded. Kuaso had been the big man in his village for many years, and was greatly honoured as an elder. The food he offered Tovo was delicious and included coffee from the high islands on the other side of the Ring, as well as a cake that must have been made with flour imported from somewhere else. Quiet shows of wealth and prestige. And honour to Tovo, of course; but mostly showing off Kuaso's success.

Kuaso had never quite forgiven Tovo for breaking it off when he had decided it was time to sail out of the Ring.

"They come back," Kuaso said, "or else they are lost."

"True," said Tovo, for it was.

Kuaso sagged and to Tovo's eyes suddenly looked old.

"What does it mean, Tovo," he whispered, "if the tana-tai is lost? What does it mean if no one is willing to hold the fire, pass it on? Two generations have grown up without ever seeing the tanà dance Aōteketētana. Nearly three."

Tovo had taught all who had come to sit at his feet as much as they could learn. The empty dancing-place on the twelfth day of the Singing of the Waters was a shame on his shoulders. He knew this.

He was as stubborn and as contrary as any Mdang born. "He will be back when it's time," he repeated, for Kuaso was an old friend but Tovo was the tanà, and he held the fire.

"I hope I live to see it," said Kuaso.

On Loaloa, his own island, he slept in his own house.

Here the questions were much more personal, though they circled on the same topic. His nieces and nephews and great-nieces and nephews asked after all their kinsmen in Gorjo City.

Kip Mdang, the one who left, was not forgotten.

"I heard he came home three times last year," someone said.

Tovo nodded, listening as his wide extended family talked over the three visits of Kip from the other side of the world.

"He didn't come out here," someone murmured.

"He hasn't been out here for years," someone else replied. Tovo watched the resignation ripple around the faces before him. "Forgotten how to speak language, no doubt."

He listened to what they did not say. *Forgotten how to*

speak language: forgotten the Lays; forgotten the lore; forgotten what it means to be an Islander.

He did not say anything. He never did, unless they asked directly, and the family had long since lost patience with his stubborn repetition that *someone always leaves.*

There was no one, bar a few elders like Kuaso, to remember when Tovo had been full of fire and ambition and the desire to see the other side of the horizon.

He knew the *Lays* with every beat of his heart, every breath of his lungs, every move of his feet in the dance. He knew that being an Islander had once meant being a sailor who thought nothing of taking a vaha across the horizon just to see what was there. They had been the great navigators, taking breadfruit and coconut and pandanus and plantains and planting them across the Wide Seas so that later voyagers would have food to eat and know that they were not the first to land there.

The Nga still Named the Stars. The Kindraa still Knew the Wind. The Nevans still Tied the Sails. The Poyë still Held the Seeds.

The Mdangs still Held the Fire.

And every time someone looked at the empty space beside him, where Kip should have been standing, Tovo smiled and said, "Someone always leaves. He'll be back when it's time."

He walked the Ring.

He touched every islet and island. He sat with elders and children, he lit fires and showed others how to light them. He sang the *Lays* and argued amicably about interpretations with those who wanted to argue. He undid the knots that were tangling up communities and helped tighten others that were loosening.

And on every island, in every village, whenever someone looked at the empty space, he smiled and said, "Someone always leaves. He'll be back when it's time."

The northern islands were generally larger, higher, more populous. Tovo walked slowly up to the heights of Orukiana, the northernmost island, climbing into the jungle where the air was cool even at noon. He listened for birds of paradise, each valley holding a different plumage, and watched warily for cassowary and the giant eagles that haunted some of the wilder peaks.

He arrived at the northern cape of the Ring at sunset and made a small camp there. He built a fire in the scorched ring of stones used by generations upon generations before him. He made it with his tovo and tanaea, which he had collected from his house on Loaloa.

The Leaping-Place for spirits going to the Ancestors was west of Loaloa, exactly opposite the Isle of the Dead following the arc of the Wake overhead. The south was the quiet realms of the gods. It was here, in the north, that the spirits of the yet-to-be-born entered the Ring.

There were others whose knowledge held secret and sacred practices to do with those young spirits coming to be born, but it had always been the practice of the tana-tai that when they walked the Ring, they spent time at Orukiana, singing the *Lays* to welcome the spirits home.

He began at the beginning, and sang through the first three of the *Lays* before dawn began to lighten the sky. It was said the spirits travelled at night, falling from the star-islands in Sky Ocean to the islands in the Wide Seas that mirrored their celestial homes.

Four nights he spent singing there, his tiny fire a bright star in the darkness, his eyes on the night sky, the shooting stars and the familiar constellations and the stars whose names he knew.

Twelve *Lays*, the twelfth so long there was talk of splitting it into a thirteenth.

They had been talking of splitting it since the Fall of Astandalas. Let the twelfth conclude with the end of the Empire, people said, and the thirteenth begin with the new order afterwards.

Such a decision could only be made by the entire conclave of the people at the Greater Singing of the Waters, when each of the lore-keepers performed their dances on the twelve successive nights of the festival.

There had not been a Greater Singing of the Waters since the Fall of Astandalas, for the tanà had not been there to dance the fire.

Lazo could not dance the fire, though he knew Aōteketē-tana, for he had a bad knee. Tovo did not have the stamina any longer for the whole dance in the full festival, when the tanà had to sing over the fire.

And Kip had not come home for the festival since he left.

It was easier to hold firm to his knowledge of Kip's stubbornness and determination when people doubted him. Up here, alone, it was harder.

Tovo sat in the cool night air, high on the cliff, looking out at the endless emptiness of the northern Wide Seas. He sang the histories of the Islanders, the familiar words friendly in his mouth, his mind, his heart, his soul.

He was not lonely. The god of mysteries was all around him, in the dark and the wind, the stars and the jungle behind him. But oh, he wished that he was not singing alone.

He remembered the boy, so angry and sharp, refusing to give in to his fear of drowning, his hatred of diving.

Tovo had seen potential in him, but he saw potential in everyone. He had thought that first dive would be the end of it: but every time Kip had cried, *I hate this!* Tovo had asked him, *Is this where you stop?*

And Kip had glared at him, so fierce and so angry and so very, very sharp, and said: *No.*

He never shouted it. He simply said *No* through gritted teeth and readied himself to dive again.

He was so brilliant. That was what Tovo always remembered: how the boy learned Islander in bare weeks, learned the *Lays* in six months, asked question after question until Tovo wanted to shake him into silence.

Look first! Listen first! Questions later! Tovo had cried, over and over again, remembering his own great-uncle saying the same to him, trying not to laugh at how much Kip was like him.

He had not been surprised when Kip left. Only that Kip had gone in a trading ship to Astandalas of the Emperors, and not in a vaha of his own hands' building to find a new island.

He walked the Ring.

He descended down through the ever-more thickly populated islands of the Eastern Ring, coming south on the arc that led back to Gorjo City. These were larger islands, higher and verdant, full of gardens and villages, some communities big enough to be called towns.

Fewer and fewer people spoke Islander as their customary speech, though even on the Epalos or Looenna there were villages where the children were knew it as their first language. Tovo drank rum and wine, foreign drinks that the people here had learned how to make, and wondered if they would understand Kip better than the people in the west.

The tana-tai was the tanà for all the Ring, east and west, Gorjo City and remotest village alike. And if the people of Loaloa, Kip's own island, did not understand him, what would it matter if the people of South Epalo did?

The elders still asked after the person who was not there, though fewer of them knew his name. Tovo told them the same answer, always the same answer.

Someone always leaves. He will come back when he's ready.

Tovo had been holding that ember for a long, long time.

Lesuia was almost the last island before he returned to Gorjo City. As he crossed the reef into the lagoon, Tovo could see the city across the bay. There were a few further uninhabited islands to visit, perhaps another three or four days of sailing, before he returned to the room he had in Lazo's house.

He was getting tired.

Not from the sailing, though he could feel that he was not as strong or as reflexive as he was. He had had good weather for his whole journey, bar a few storms he had sat out on various islands, but if an unexpected squall had blown up he might well have found it difficult to respond.

It was, of a certainty, the last time he would sail his vaha alone around the Ring.

Lesuia was a medium-sized island for this part of the Ring, with five or six villages. Tovo made his way to Ikiano, where his second sister's granddaughter had married a local man and now lived.

Aya welcomed him warmly, taking him into her house, introducing her children and giving him a comfortable seat on her porch. He accepted the coffee and city-style sweet pastries she offered him, and talked to her children about how to light and tend a fire.

Her husband was off fishing, Aya told him, and in due course sent her children off to play with their cousins.

Tovo set down his bowl of coffee and waited patiently for the inevitable question.

Aya was young—hardly past thirty—and had been one of those who had sat at Tovo's feet for a time.

She had had the talent, but not the drive, to be the tanà. She had not learned the whole of the fire dance, though she knew the *Lays*, and she held the fire here on this side of the Ring. Tovo rather thought that over the decades, as she grew in knowledge and wisdom, she would end up in a position similar to Lazo's in Gorjo City.

If Kip were truly lost, Lazo would likely ask Aya to hold the full dances and pass them on. It had been known to happen before, when a family narrowed down and the knowledge was in danger of being forgotten. Tovo's great-niece Vinyë had held the dances of her husband's family in trust for her children, because he had been the last of his maternal line.

There were so many Mdangs in the younger generations: Kuaso's questions about what it meant for the Islands as a whole if none of them felt able to Hold the Fire hit hard.

Tovo sat there with Aya's coffee. He was not disappointed in her. There had never been many called to being the tanà: for there to be three in five generations was not unusual.

If there were still the third.

Aya poured Tovo more coffee. They sat together on the mats she had placed on the platform in front of her house. They faced not the centre of the village, but instead through a thin screen of trees the clear water of the lagoon. Far out near the barrier reef was Aya's husband on a small outrigger canoe. He cut a fine traditional figure, with the claw-shaped sail of the Eastern Ring silhouetted against the sky, his net casting glittering droplets of water as he raised and cast it out again.

"I do not remember Kip coming to Loaloa," Aya said presently. "I was too young. He had gone to Astandalas before I paid any attention."

Tovo nodded silently, listening. Of course Aya would begin with the missing Kip. She was very close to being the tanà of the northern Ring, as Lazo was in Gorjo City. Perhaps she was ready to learn a few more of the dances, another layer or two of the lore. It had not been for her when she was in her teens, but that did not mean it would never be for her.

"There were many stories of him on Loaloa."

Aya looked sidelong at him, and her sober expression puckered into a bright grin. Tovo smiled back. There *were* many stories about Kip on Loaloa. He had thrown himself into everything whole-heartedly.

Everything. *Everything*.

"When I met Cliopher Mdang here with his Shaian lord," she said, "I did not realize it was the same man. I thought it was another one of the cousins. He did not seem much like the stories."

"Mmm."

Aya offered him the plate of tarts. When he declined, she set the plate down beside her, her expression a curious one.

"Something happened when he was here," she said. "I have not known what to think of it. Then we went to Solaara, Jiano and I, to talk to the Lord Emperor about the fish farm."

Tovo nodded to show he knew of this journey.

"Someone always leaves," Aya said, her eyes on her husband out on the reef. "We all want to be Elonoa'a, don't we? If only the emperors were ever Aurelius Magnus, and worth sailing out of the world to find ... Oh, Buru Tovo, I had never understood that passage in the *Lays* before."

He looked at her. *Listen first.*

She glanced quickly at him and then down again, cheeks flushing. "I have often wondered what Elonoa'a's family thought. Someone always leaves ... and it is always the best, the brightest, the star we all want to see shine, isn't it? They could not have been happy when Elonoa'a took ship after the emperor. I have often thought of it."

Tovo nodded. He too had often thought of that passage of

the *Lays*. Kip had been fascinated by the story, had asked everyone he could find for every version of the stories, every snippet caught in another tale, every rumour passed down in a family.

"When we went to Solaara, we found that the Lord Emperor is the fire at the centre of the court. Everyone circling around him, everyone dancing around that fire, the hearth at the centre of the world."

She dropped her hand to fiddle with the fringe on the hem of her sarong. "Cliopher didn't dance around the centre. He stood beside him."

Tovo hummed acknowledgement, placing this into his knowledge of Kip.

"When I saw him, I thought he was the tanà for the whole world."

Tovo felt his breath stop, just for a moment, at that soft statement. Aya had studied the *Lays*; she was a wise woman for her age, shining brilliant. She would be a great elder when her time came.

Look first. Listen first.

There was a time for questions; that was where Kip had always fallen down. Either he asked too many or not enough.

"What makes you say that?" he asked, neither eager nor angry, simply questioning.

Aya leaned back against the post holding up the palm-frond roof. She closed her eyes. "There was a market in Ikiava when he was here, Cliopher and his lord and the others. I liked his friends," she added. "I thought his lord was Fitzroy Angursell." She paused. "I still think he's Fitzroy Angursell."

The name was foreign and unfamiliar. "Who is he, then?"

Aya grinned, her eyes laughing. "A rather infamous poet from just before Artorin Damara took the throne."

"What kind of poet?"

"A very good one. Funny, sharp, political, sometimes very beautiful."

"Kip would like that."

Aya held still for a moment. "Would he?"

He remembered that boy, so sharp, so brilliant, so angry, sometimes feeling so strongly he cried with his passion. "Yes."

"I think I'm right," she murmured. "He didn't exactly *deny* it."

Tovo waited for her to circle back to her main point. He had nowhere to be, nothing to do, but sit here and listen to her talk.

It was easy listening to her when she spoke to the deepest desires of his own heart. He would not pretend otherwise. He was the tana-tai, who showed the people what it meant to be them. He would not lie to himself.

"There was a market," she repeated. "We—Jiano and I— we invited Cliopher and his lord and their friends to come with us. Cliopher wore city clothes, not proper finery, and I remembered some of the things people say, that he's forgotten what it is to be an Islander."

And if the tanà—the one everyone expected to be the next tana-tai—had forgotten that, what did it mean, what could it mean, for the rest of them?

"I have lived here for a few years now, but there are still people who live on the outlying islands I do not know. There was an old man who came selling shells. He had splendid efela." She touched one of her own efela, a beautiful piece of green coral set on a simple braided line. "I traded one of my books—I write stories—for this one."

"A good trade," Tovo said, leaning forward to examine the efela more carefully. It was a beautiful piece, the green coral threaded with blue and something nearly silver. He'd never seen the coloration before, and admired it.

"I thought so." Aya hesitated, then laughed haltingly, as if her thoughts were stealing the breath from her. "I went on, around the corner, but I was within sight when Cliopher—Kip—came to the seller. I looked back when he stopped, wondering what he would choose, what he would trade."

Tovo held still. Choosing an efela was a matter of great import; what one traded for it even more so.

"Kip lifted up a long chain of golden shells I am sure was not there when I'd looked. They caught the sun: they were so beautiful. And such a long strand. I would have seen the shells if they'd been there when I'd been looking. The efelauni didn't have so many as all that."

"I understand," he murmured. There were stories in the *Lays*—and even more stories of the sort aunties told the children—about magical or mystical purveyors of efela. *Efelauni*, as they said in the Western Ring, the word Aya was using. An ordinary trader in shells and efela would be called a posao, after the posà of the Walea, those who Held the Efela. Any posao was on the edge of mystery. The efelauni *were* mysteries.

Tovo had seen and heard many things in his life. He did not discount possibilities no matter how far-fetched they seemed. He had met the gods walking the islands.

"The efelauni said—oh, it was all out of the *Lays*, Buru Tovo. He said, 'Your hands know what your eyes are seeing.' And Cliopher said, 'You know how it is, I was taught by my great-uncle.'" Something like that ... his words are not so clear in my mind."

"I understand," he said again. No, they wouldn't be. Not if this was what he suspected it was.

Oh, what a thing to imagine, if it was what he suspected it was!

"He asked, the efelauni asked Cliopher the questions out of the *Lays*: 'What is your name? Your island? Your dances?' And Cliopher looked like—he looked as if he had stepped out of one of the *Lays* himself. He lifted his chin and he said, 'I am

Cliopher Mdang of Tahivoa. My island is Loaloa. My dances are Aōteketētana.'"

Aōteketētana. Not *Aōtetana.* Not simply the fire dances, but the Fire Dance.

Aya opened her eyes to smile at him. Her eyes were shining with tears. "I always wanted someone to ask me that," she whispered. "Jiano did, when I was sailing around the Ring and I came to the reef here ..." She waved out at her husband, who was moving along the inner line of the reef, a fishing spear in his hand, his nets once more in the water. "He was there on the inside in his canoe, and I on the outside in mine, and we looked at each other across the coral—and he asked me those questions, and I knew he was mine."

Tovo had wanted to be asked those questions, too. Even in his youth they had not been common. You asked them when the answer was meaningful: when you wanted to enter yourself and the person in front of you into legend, into the world of the *Lays.*

"I don't think Cliopher knew he had switched into language, he was so focused on the efelauni. No hesitation in him, his voice, his body. And then the efelauni said, 'I have heard of three sons of Vonou'a.'"

Tovo's attention sharpened, though he kept his body loose. Anyone who remembered Kip as a youth remembered how he had either sought every possible story about Elonoa'a and Aurelius Magnus, or about the three sons of Vonou'a.

Aya's voice dropped. "Cliopher said, 'I went to sit at the feet of the Sun.'" There was no hesitation now as she recounted Kip's words: these were writ on her mind as sharply as the words of the efelauni out of the stories.

Her voice dropped again, with wonder and a certain shivering awe. "And the efelauni asked him, 'What will you bring home to the Islands?'"

Only one efelauni would dare ask that. Tovo caught his

breath, unashamed to admit his interest, his intense desire to hear the answer.

"It was out of the *Lays*," Aya said again. "It should be *in* the *Lays*, Buru Tovo. It was a market like any other market, nothing of note except for the velioi guests ... and yet it was then, there, here, now, that the gods asked a question."

"And what did he answer?"

Aya swallowed. Her eyes were even brighter, and her hands were trembling. Tovo leaned forward and captured her hands with his. Her fingers were very cold, and curved in his gentle grip.

"Buru Tovo," she said, "he said, 'I will bring home the hearthfire of a new life for the world.' Just—just like that."

Tovo thought of those words, the valence of them in the Islander language. To bring home a tanaea—oh, not too many knew of the striking rock's proper name.

But *ta*, life, everyone knew that was related to *tana*, fire. And what word could the Islanders use for 'the world' bar 'the horizon around my island'?

The hearthfire of a new life. The spark of a new fire. The fire of a new life to the horizon around my island.

Aya spoke again, her voice low, certain, awed. "He looked straight at the efelauni and he said that, as if he had never doubted, never wavered, never once stepped aside from the ke'ea. 'I will bring a new fire to the hearth of the world.' As if ..."

As if Kip had decided at the age of twelve to be tanà, and followed that calling wherever it led him, refusing to take the ke'ea that others claimed was the true one unless he had decided it was also his.

The tanà knew the *Lays*, all the cycle and stories of them. Knew the interpretations that had been given in the past, the knowledge of those who went before. Could hold the heart of the community, light the fire and tend it.

The tana-tai took the *Lays* and said: here we are, here is where we have been, here is where we can go.

"I will bring a new fire to the hearth of the world," she murmured. Jiano turned, dove down, sleek as a dolphin, his spear a line of silver. Aya sighed. "I couldn't help but stare. The efelauni looked up and he caught my eyes and he laughed—laughed like a kookaburra—laughed like—"

Like Vou'a, Tovo finished, naming the Son of Laughter, the god of mysteries, the trickster. Once he himself had met that god, been asked those questions from out of the *Lays*.

Oh, that was long ago now, and Tovo had traded a different promise—not for an efela of shining golden shells but a mystery he had never finished plumbing.

"And Cliopher looked so embarrassed I could not say anything," Aya said. "That is the moment you skip in a story ... the *Lays* do not describe the arguments Elonoa'a must have had with his family when he set off to sail out of the world for Aurelius Magnus."

2

Tovo returned to Gorjo City at dusk, sliding into the city as the lights rose wavering over the waters of canals and lagoons.

At the edge of the city he crossed the row of buoys marking the route the sea train took when it arrived. They were lit, burning with a fierce green magic, showing that the sea train was coming in. He moved his canoe out of the way, anchoring it at the lighthouse at the end of the breakwater that formed the quay where the sea train would stop.

He had seen the velioi marvel from a distance, but never close to. He waited as the night fell, the blue dusk shimmering around him, the air full of flowers and the scents of the city. Food and people and stone and seaweed and all the other familiar crush of things.

The train was illuminated with golden lanterns. Tovo watched the water spray up in two fine spumes, catching the lights and falling back down in white and golden glitter against the dark water.

It was quietly musical, humming deep-down at a level that thrummed in the stone of the breakwater. Tovo sat on the bench at the lighthouse, watching the train's lights resolve into little chains of illuminated balls, windows bright with magic, people standing, gathering their things, peering out at the city coming to meet them.

He waved at a small child peering out as the train slowed and went past him. The child waved back, face thrown back with joy, just a moment before they were gone and past.

There were six compartments, each of them like the belly of a ship. No sail, but a sense of magic rushing past him. The wake washed up against the stones and made his vaha rock.

Tovo waited until the train came to a stop, and then he went down and untied his vaha and sailed slowly down the other side of the breakwater, watching people get off with their families and belongings, watching them meet those who had come surging out of the city to greet them.

Aya had said it was a way to cross the world if one wasn't prepared to sail the old way and didn't want to go with the traders.

Tovo had not thought he would leave the circle of the Ring again, not before he went to the Isle of the Dead and then followed the Wake to the jumping-off place of the spirits. He had thought he would hold his small ember of hope that Kip would come back when it was time, until it was his own time to go.

He had, at some level, given up.

Tovo looked at the train, this new and grand thing, which Aya said Kip had caused to happen.

Someone always left. Sometimes they were lost, and did not come back. Other times they came back with a striking rock, and started a new fire.

He could keep waiting, as he had been waiting for years, for Kip's sail to come back over the horizon.

He was getting old. It would be good to *know*.

And, if he were honest with himself, he wanted to see the other side of the horizon again.

Aya had said there would be two days before the train turned to go back across the Wide Seas to the velioi lands.

Tovo had been known to go voyaging with less notice.

~

It *was* easy.

He went first to one of the government offices he'd never felt much need to visit before, where for the first time in his life he handled money.

That was Kip's doing too, Aya had said. He'd made it so anyone who needed money could have some.

Tovo had never bothered to learn all the nuances of money, but he knew that was a new thing, and he was proud that it was because of Kip that he would be able to go so quietly, as easily as if he were using his own skills and knowledge to ready his canoe. He had sailed the Ring in his ninetieth year; he had nothing to prove now.

He took the money to the office at the head of the train, where he bought a berth—just like a Shaian ship, so strict and orderly, but never mind that—for the journey east.

"I want to go to Solaara," he said.

The officer nodded. "When you get to Csiven you can ask the officials there how to get the rest of the way."

He accepted this, and on their recommendation collected his dominoes, a bag of his favourite foods, and a blanket for cool evenings. He took his vaha to a quiet covered berth he knew would be out of the way, for he did not like to leave his vaha so long in the sun as it would be outside Lazo's, and after he gathered all of his necessities together in his bilum, not forgetting his tovo and tanaea, he returned with his ticket to the train.

The official's expressions were amusing when he arrived, still in his traditional skirt because why did he need to change? He was going to see his apprentice, his kinsman, his great-nephew who had sat at his feet until he knew the entire cycle of the *Lays* backwards and forwards in Shaian and in language.

His apprentice who had never claimed anything in the hearing of anyone in the Ring, except when he was asked who he was by one of the gods.

Well, that was a pattern in the *Lays*, too, even if not the one anyone would expect of the outspoken Kip.

Tovo knew what the air felt like across the entirety of the Wide Seas. In his youth he had sailed the Sociable Isles, all the archipelagoes named in the *Lays*.

The train's route went that way, they said. He knew the names they mentioned, and was eager to see those islands again. He had not thought he would.

So: dominoes, a blanket, a bag of food that would keep. There was food to be bought on the train, they told him, even on the long stretch between Gorjo City and Isiguro, the next inhabited island out.

Tovo remembered when there had been other villages between the Vangavaye-ve and Isiguro, but they had faded in the last years of the Empire, and disappeared completely in the terrible years after the Empire had gone away again. There had been storms across the Wide Seas, flooding islands that had always been precarious.

He settled into his berth, which consisted of a kind of bed that folded down from the wall, a table and a stool that tucked under the bed when it was down or were usable during the day when it was up, and a window out the side to watch the world go by.

At the end of each compartment was a little bath-house and a privy, one at each end. There was a sign informing them of the rules—don't take too long in the bathhouse, bear in mind the others in your compartment, clean up after yourself. The attendant in charge of the train read them out to him in slow, loud tones.

Tovo nodded, grinning amicably at him. He could read Shaian but did not find much call to do so. And of course there would be rules, that was a Shaian thing. They always wanted rules, strict and strict.

A small child was watching carefully as the attendant showed him the facilities and pointed to the last compartment on the train as being the one with food and water. Tovo thanked the attendant politely enough; he was a velioi and clearly didn't know what to make of Tovo, but that was fine. He had the taste of magic around him, related to the magic of the train; probably he helped with it.

"They told me the same thing," the child said once the attendant had reiterated the fact that the roof was open but safety was their own concern. Tovo thought this perhaps a little exaggerated, as there were rails all around, and a movable wind-and-sun screen. "If I fall off, it's my own fault and they won't come get me."

Tovo smiled down at the child, who was half-velioi by her features. She had one blue eye and one brown, and her Islander-gold skin had paler patches around her mouth and eyes, white flashes in her hair. On her hands the patches looked rather like the reflection of ripples on leaves overhanging water.

Tovo liked how she grinned up at him, and nodded seriously back at her. "You'll have to make sure not to fall off, then."

She wrinkled her nose thoughtfully. "Or make sure I fall off *with* a boat."

"You'd want more than a boat, to sail the middle of the Wide Seas."

"Leave the gentleman alone," a harassed woman said,

hastening up with a wild look in her eyes to grab the child's arm. "I'm sorry, sir, she's—"

"Oh, not doing any harm. Tovo inDaino of Loaloa," he said, smiling at the child and then at her mother.

"I'm Tanaea," the child informed him, and with the child's unerring instinct for saying a true thing at precisely the wrong moment, added, "because mum says I am her little hearth-fire. Not because we're Mdangs!" She laughed heartily at her own joke.

"Oh, *Tanaea*," her mother said, her eyes flicking to Tovo's efetana. "I'm Guite ke'e Nuarafo, sir."

"Well, I *am* a Mdang," Tovo replied, grinning down at the girl, who must have been eight or so. "In fact, I am the tanà of the Mdangs, which means I Hold the Fire, so I think we shall get along famously. Tanaea means hearthfire, but it has another meaning too. When you make a fire, you know, you can use a tovo—that's me—and a tanaea—that's you—to light the spark."

Tanaea stared up at him, mouth open a little with delight. "Are they rocks? Like flint and steel?"

Smart girl. "Yes," Tovo said.

"Do you have some?"

Tovo grinned. "I do."

He nodded at her mother, who was regarding him with surprise and as if she were trying to remember something she'd once heard.

"The tanà holds the fire," he said. "Your daughter is safe with me. Are you in this compartment? We'll be together at least as far as Isiguro, then."

"We're going to Epapapapalona," Tanaea informed him. "Mum says it's weeks and weeks away. Are you going that far?"

"I am going all the way to Solaara."

"To see the Emperor?"

Tovo grinned, thinking of what Aya had said, that Kip had

gone as Elonoa'a had gone, to stand beside his emperor. "I expect so."

~

Tanaea was a splendid apprentice. She asked questions—so many questions—but she listened reasonably well to the answers, which was more than Tovo could say of certain other people.

The roof had a splendid view. It was higher than he was accustomed to from the deck of a vaha but not so high as from one of the Shaian-style trading ships. Nor, of course, the flying ships that they saw in the distance once or twice.

He spent most of his time up there, with the wind in his face and the sea to the horizon and the sun on his back. It was, he thought, good.

Tanaea joined him for most of it, forever chased by her mother with hat and some sort of ointment to block the sun.

"It's my spots," she told Tovo the first day, with a long-suffering air, tying the hat under her chin so the wind wouldn't steal it. Guite hovered until Tovo waved her off. Tanaea's mother did not like being on the roof, not at all. "They burn really fast. They're called vitiligo."

"Are they?"

"Mum says the gods touched me in the womb, but dad said that his auntie had them too. And besides, it didn't show up until I was *five*."

"What do you think?"

Tanaea spread out her fingers and pondered the patterns there. "I think the gods probably have better things to do than go round poking babies, don't you?"

"You'd be surprised," Tovo murmured, and then had to tell Tanaea story after story of the gods. She told him some back, some she'd heard in other places, and some she'd made up. Her father was a writer, a maker of stories in the same way Aya was, and Tanaea was already starting to imitate him. A good apprentice, indeed.

She was particularly interested in how the sea train worked, and kept asking the attendants for more details.

Tovo gave her some advice on talking to people and was delighted when she came back with the revelation she'd managed to get an invitation to the pilot's cabin.

"The train has a special magic fire in its belly," she told him after her visit there.

"Does it?"

"Yes, and Captain Kuuli says that it takes in the sea-water and turns it into fresh water and steam by the magic fire, and that's what makes it go. But it needs to follow the line of the tracks, otherwise it loses the connection to the magic of the Lights."

"How interesting."

"Yes. The magic is all sparkly."

"Is it?"

"Yes, it tastes like books."

"How do you mean? I don't have any magic," he said seriously, "so you shall have to explain to me."

"My daddy writes books, about people and places where we go. We travel a lot, you see. He's in Epapapapalona, but it's very very small, and mum said that since he wanted to be there *all* through the rainy season because they do something special there, the people, that meant we could go on the train to visit Grandmum and Grandpapa and all my cousins."

"A capital idea," Buru acknowledged.

"My daddy says all books are special and have magic in them, because words can do all sorts of things, but *I* think some books are *more* special than others. Some books are magic. They fizz. Like the train."

Tovo considered this. There was magic, of course. The

kind the Astandalans had used was as common a skill amongst the Islanders as it was with anyone else: about as common as a gift for any other art, and with as much a range of talent and skill.

And then there was old magic. That had always been rare.

But there were stories. Most of them involved someone with eyes that were noticeably a bit *different*. He had always thought that had more to do with what such mages saw, or at least what they looked at, but perhaps the *Lays* were a touch more literal than that.

Tovo smiled down at Tanaea, with her one blue eye and her one brown one, and began telling her some of the old tales of people who could speak to the winds or understand the whales or call up fish or fire.

He was the tanà. When he saw a spark of something good, it was his duty to nourish it.

The weeks passed, quietly and pleasantly. Tanaea had started to ask for Islander words by their second or third day, and by the end of the two months they spent together she had a solid grasp of language and was well on her way to knowing the central *Lays* by heart.

Even though he did not have the usual constellations of signs to orient him—on the train he could not feel the deep currents and changes in the swell, nor taste the saltiness of the water, and even the wind was less informative without a sail to help him touch it—he was nonetheless able to hold his island in his mind and keep a rough sense of where in the Wide Seas they were.

One night he realized they were crossing that mysterious central space beloved of Vou'a, where the viau would run.

He told Tanaea and her mother Guite, and the other

passengers in their compartment, who by this point had all come to realize he might be very much an Outer Ring Islander but that merely meant he knew the Wide Seas better than any of them. After taking a sunset meal with Tanaea and Guite he led them up to the roof.

The indigo sky was velvety. The sea was a deep, lustrous blue, green phosphorescence in the wake of the train, rolling back on either side of its bow carriage, very still and steady and reflecting the stars and viau in their magnificence.

"What are they?" Guite asked, as the flashes of brilliance streaked through the sky above them. "Shooting stars?"

"Viau," Tovo answered. "Maybe. They belong here."

The viau were at their finest; they always were, he thought, when someone was seeing them for the first time. They could be seen from land, but never so well as in the open.

He'd heard that they were not visible away from the Wide Seas, that people elsewhere could only see a handful of shooting stars, not the actual, proper viau, the great schools of white-and-gold streaks and sparks that lit the sky once or twice a decade across the whole breadth of the ocean, and more often than that if you were in the right part of the sea.

It was a sight Tovo had seen many times, and never found tiresome. He had first come across it on his way home from his great journey, when he'd been pushed far to the east of his homeward course by a storm, and ended up in the northern part of this sea, where no one ever went on purpose.

If you chased the viau, as the saying went, you were a fool, heading into the uninhabited parts of the ocean.

If you *followed* the viau, on the other hand, you might find the island in the centre of the Wide Seas where Vou'a was known to dwell.

It was like a sardine run following the line of the Wake across the sky. There was an old, old story that the viau were the fish the Ancestors sought, their nets splashing down and scattering their prey so they flashed through the living world.

Tanaea was entranced, laying beside him for hours after everyone else had gone back to their berths. "This is magic," she whispered, almost rigid with her own intensity. "This is what magic is *like*. This is—it *is*—and surely, surely I can find it again, can't I, Buru Tovo?"

Tovo stared up at the sky, the stars and the Wake and the viau in their masses, evanescent as a fountain of sparks when you thrust a log onto a fire.

"You can," he said quietly, "if you are willing to run after it."

"I am," Tanaea said. Her voice sounded thick with tears, but she was staring open-eyed and fiercely at the sky. "I *am*."

"People say *chasing a viau* when they mean someone is being foolish, silly," he warned her.

He had been telling her stories from the *Lays* these past weeks, story after story of those who heard a rumour from the sea of a new island, or a message from a bird of a new food, or a chorus from the coral itself singing of its beauty.

"It can't be silly to follow something that beautiful, can it?" she said.

"No," he replied quietly, feeling her small hand steal into his. "No."

"I'm not sure I can ever thank you enough," Tanaea's mother said to him, the night after the viau.

"For what?"

"For ... everything." Guite rubbed her face with her hands. She looked much calmer and happier than she had when they'd first embarked, her eyes brighter, her skin clearer, her smile easier. "Tanaea adores talking with you so much."

"She's a splendid apprentice for a season."

"We're not Mdang, for you to teach her."

"With a name like that?" He laughed. "It doesn't matter. I give the fire to all who need it or want it."

"She's so smart," her mother said, sighing. "Oh, I shouldn't say this, but I needed the break so much. To know that she's safe with you—not just safe but *learning* so much—she comes back telling me about the wind and the waves and the names of all the things we can see, and the *Lays* ... My granny used to sing them to me, but I didn't remember them enough to teach to her. Thank you."

"You've raised a splendid daughter," he said. "Anyone would be proud to teach her—and to learn from her."

"She does like to share," her mother said, laughing weakly. "You've had ... a son, maybe, like that? A grandson?"

"A great-nephew," Tovo answered.

And then, because Tanaea was off reading a book, something she enjoyed when the afternoon sun was too strong for her, Tovo sat down with her mother and told her stories of Kip and the splendid man he had become.

They reached Epapalona—Tovo rather preferred Tanaea's version—and parted ways.

Tovo had taught Tanaea the words for a farewell, and the words too for a greeting after a long absence: *Tē ke'e'vina-tē zēnava parahë'ala*, which meant something like 'How splendid that the star-paths of our voyages meet here!'

The response was: *Tō mo'ea-tō avivayë o rai'ivayë*: 'New islands and old islands are ours to discover now we are together again.'

Tanaea murmured the words over to herself as they

watched the dock at Epapalona come closer. "Will we meet again, Buru Tovo?" she asked.

"No one can answer that," he replied gently. "If not in this world, our spirits may meet as we sail Sky Ocean in the next."

"Can I write to you?"

Tovo's only correspondent was Kip, who wrote to everybody. He was rather tickled at the idea that his chance-met apprentice might be the second. "You can," he said, and met Guite's startled glance with a grin. "Send it to Lazo Mdang in Gorjo City, I''ll get it from him eventually. Probably be pretty slow writing back, I don't do it much."

"We move around a lot so letters are always slow," Guite said, though her eyes were on the velioi man standing on the platform, his pale skin shaded by a wide-brimmed straw hat very like Tanaea's.

"Kip will know how to reach you, wherever you are," Tovo said, nodding. "That's the sort of thing he's good at. You write, Tanaea, and I'll write back. We'll see what sparks we can make together."

"Good fires," she said, firmly, as firmly as a promise to the gods.

"They're the best kind," he agreed.

The train slowed to a halt, and those who were leaving gathered up their things. Tanaea gave him a hug around the middle and grinned through her tears as she caught sight of her father, who was waving madly at them.

Tovo smiled and waved good-bye as the train started off again. He might see Tanaea again, or then again he might not. He hoped so: she had been a delight, and her name *was* a good omen, surely. A bit of a joke from the Son of Laughter, but that was a gift, too.

He settled back in his berth after greeting the newcomers to the train. One or other of them might be interested in playing dominoes, telling over some new stories, perhaps a variant of the *Lays* from this part of the Wide Seas.

Plenty to think about. Albeit Tovo's thoughts were turning evermore to the east, and the emperor who had been great enough to keep a Mdang at his side for all these years.

~

Csiven was a large city, full of bustle and noise.

It was a city of merchants and traders, busy as a market-day in the trading season. After so long in the narrow confines of the sea train, Tovo rather enjoyed his few nights in the city. He had talked to the people who got on the sea train closer to its end point—it was much more used as a means of local transport, the eastern side of Jilkano—and had determined the location of a couple of wontok, the cousins of a man from the train.

The cousins were from one of the Sociable Isles and had long since forgotten any Islander they knew, but Tovo had met their grandfather in his own youthful travels, and could tell them stories in return for their hospitality. They put him onto the barge that went up a long series of canals and locks into and then through the mountains to the plains on the other side.

It was a strange sort of boat, the barge, flat-bottomed and blunt-nosed, and it was drawn by teams of animals on shore. Mules, he learned when he asked what they were. He stared at them openly. For all his travels upon the Wide Seas he had never gone farther than a day or two's walk from the shore before. The animals of the large continents were strange marvels to him.

The canal, a human-made river, was made to be flat. When it came to the mountains it was lifted up in an ingenious arrangement of levers and doors that Tovo thought Tanaea would have enjoyed learning about very much. Kip too; but he probably *did* know about them.

There were a lot of people talking about Cliopher Mdang out here in the wide world, that was for sure.

Tovo sat on the deck and watched the water fill the basin and lift the barge up, step by step as they went lock by lock, until they could go straight through a pass in the mountains and start descending the other side.

It was, he supposed, faster than going all the way around the southern tip of Southern Dair, with all the storms and sudden fogs and dangerous magic and monsters of the southern ocean.

And it was not *entirely* boring. It stopped to load and unload cargo frequently, and there were always people clustered close with trade-goods. He ignored most of these, although he did buy a brightly coloured cape—a poncho, he was told it was called—of finely woven wool, because high up in the mountains it *was* cold at night.

These mountains were not like a high island's peak, green with jungle, but were grey and rocky. Their deep valleys had jungle, mist rising; from rivers far, far down under the canopy. There were rope bridges extending from peak to peak, joining them together. Tovo looked at people crossing the bridges, sometimes with strange animals bearing burdens led behind them, and marvelled at how wide the world was.

The stars were clear, and he looked up, often, at the great arc of the Wake. His destination lay along that line, even if the barge necessarily cut counter to the exact arc. Often enough one had to tack back and forth to reach one's goal. Any sailor knew that; not all of them remembered to apply it to other parts of their lives.

～

There were jungles on the eastern side, full of huge and colourful relatives of the familiar parrots and cockatoos of home. Tovo enjoyed watching them, blue-and-yellow and green-and-red and some splendid and truly enormous black ones. There were any number of smaller birds, and trees and vines and shrubs and flowers beyond counting.

The canal took him eventually to a river, where the barge-master told him to transfer to another vessel, a riverboat, which would take him to the coast—the *Eastern* ocean, the far side of the world indeed!—and another sea train north.

Tovo considered how often Kip had made this trip, in the days before he could come on the fancy flying ships, and was privately impressed.

Though of course it always mattered most *why* anyone did what they did. What stories did Kip tell of his journeys? That was what Tovo had come to hear.

Look first, listen first ... and questions later, too.

Down the river, the Orcholon, where huge grey beasts with snake-like noses and sail-like ears stood washing themselves in the shallows. All the animals seemed larger-than-life: the parrots, the *elephants*, the river-monsters who lay with only their eyes and nostrils above the surface, floating plants disguising their bodies, watching the boat as it went past with hungry eyes.

Jilkano was said to have crocodiles, big ones, on its northern coasts, but Tovo had not seen them. He saw the ones on the Orcholon, however. The ship went down another lock and then sailed ponderously down the wide, slow, murky river, full of islands that were themselves full of birds in their trees and crocodiles on the banks.

These crocodiles were white like bleached coral. At first

Tovo thought they were dead as white coral, but they were not; they were simply white.

He did not go swimming in this river. He had not reached his ninetieth year and travelled more than halfway around the world to be eaten by a crocodile!

They went past a great city, with terraced towers and elephants seemingly everywhere. There were many monkeys, too, as he was told they were called: disquietingly like human children, but furred and with long grasping tails and faces that showed cunning but no true intelligence.

They must be sacred to the gods here, along with those striking white crocodiles, Tovo thought, and made a small offering to his own god Vou'a, god of mysteries.

After restocking in the city the river-boat continued down through swamps full of trees with aerial roots reaching down. Tovo watched the many creatures in the trees—the mangroves, he learned—birds, monkeys, crocodiles, and strange fish that jumped up and sunned themselves on the branches from time to time.

And then there was fresh salt air, and a new ocean Tovo had never seen from this side: the Eastern Sea of Zunidh according to the emperors, the Other Side of the Horizon for the Islanders. He was well pleased to touch its water, taste its salt, feel its rhythms and currents.

North on another train, chugging along close to the shore, stopping at many small villages and towns along the coast. There were islands out to sea, cloud-wreathed high islands. One was black and bare, disturbing at even this remove. An island cursed, clearly. Tovo saw how the others on the train averted their eyes from the burned island, or made some sign or other if they happened to catch sight of it, and instead of asking anyone about it he made another prayer to Vou'a to ease whatever shadow that place still cast.

And still he travelled.

He was not unfamiliar with long, long voyages, solitary or with a crew. Once he had not thought much of crossing to the Isolates or Turtle Island or one of the nearer archipelagos when the mood took him, and those would take six months or a year for the round trip. He had grown soft over the years, he decided, let his horizon shrink to the compass of the Ring.

It was a goodly size, the Ring of the Vangavaye-ve, but the world was much wider than that. It was good to be reminded.

Everywhere he went, no matter how wide the world was, he heard rumours of Kip. Even without whatever else he had done, that money-store of his had changed a lot of people's lives.

At nearly the very end of the fourth month of his journey, Tovo reached Port Ithazhi and was directed to another river-boat. His store of money had had to be replenished once already, in Csiven before he had embarked on the barge-canal, and he did so again in the port. The wide world was much more expensive than it had been in his youth.

Of course, he had not had to try all the different foods of all the different vendors crowding onto the train or the river-barges at each stop, either. And the barges and trains were not free for his own limbs' labour and knowledge, as his vaha was.

Tovo folded his bright poncho and set it into the bilum he'd brought from home, along with the tapa-cloth pouch in which he kept his money. He had a few new kinds of fruit to try on this barge, and some unfamiliarly-spiced fish jerky, and that would suit him well enough, he reckoned.

Upriver against the current they went, the boat's broad triangular sails catching the wind. There were reed-plains on the northern side of the river, with a weight to them. Tovo found himself wondering what Tanaea would have thought of them, with her sense for the deeper magic of things.

They passed through a gap between two ridges that stood out of the plains like walls, and there in front of him Tovo finally saw the city of Solaara, with its white Palace high on its hill gleaming in the sunlight like a viau come to rest.

3

It was late afternoon when he arrived, and the city was large. Tovo was unaccustomed to such places, and although he knew he should aim uphill he found the streets slanting off in all sorts of directions.

He ended up in a green area of some form. Maybe a place like the one at the top of Mama Ituri's Son back home—a refuge for people who wanted green space but didn't want to leave the city, an absurdity in his mind but what did he know, anyway. This one made a bit more sense. Big city, made sense people needed the green. There was a market going on, with musicians and people selling all sorts of strange foods.

Tovo wandered along, listening to the music—he liked the people drumming with tuned steel drums, the notes sounding forth sweet and clear—and tried a few different foods. Fried things, sweet things, something crunchy and salty, something soft that made his teeth stick together.

By the time he had unstuck his teeth it was dark, and the market lights had come on bright. These were magic, soft and pleasant on the eyes. They made the place seem even more vibrant, as people appeared out of the darkness and the conversations and music both got louder. He found himself a tree and squatted down under it, enjoying the festive atmosphere.

Eventually the crowds dispersed, but there didn't seem to be any particular reason to go anywhere else—and it was probably rude to call on Kip so late—so Tovo tucked himself behind the tree, where a thicket made a cozy, protected space, and slept well with his head pillowed on his bag.

In the morning he found a public fountain and an early-rising coffee stall, and having washed his face and hands and drunk down a cup of strong, foreign coffee—good, mind you, for all that it was clearly a different kind than he was used to— even after the sea train's many varieties—and with a helpful set of directions from the coffee vendor, ambled up to the Palace.

He didn't like the look of the front doors. Too big, too grand, too much for show. Doors for Big Men, or those who wanted to be noticed by Big Men.

Still, the big open area in front of the front doors was a fine dancing-ground, or would be if the sun wasn't so hot here, and after tapping the stones with his feet, nimbly performing a handful of steps, Tovo felt he had greeted the building well enough to be acquainted.

Vangavayen Islanders only made a few longhouses, but all houses were said to have guardian spirits, ancestors perhaps who sat watch over their descendants. It was only polite to greet them, even if one of the other doors would be the one for him.

Tovo went off to the left, following one of the long arms of stone that reached out from the central building. There were gardens clustered close, expanding all over the crest of the steep hill they had built on. He recognized a few of the plants, and noted with approval that there were plenty of food plants here as well as ones just for decoration. Not that there was anything wrong with liking pretty things around you, that was half the point of life, after all—making your surroundings a little prettier for yourself and your kin and community—but it was good not to forget about the practical things.

And good, too, to look on so useful a plant as a banana tree and see beauty as well use. Tovo was quietly pleased.

The palace seemed to be built like a sea star, which seemed a bit strange—but who was he to judge the ways of velioi? He walked through the gardens, peering up at the even ranks of windows, noticing the many doors, looking out as the path brought him to the edge of the hill out over the city and river-valley down below. He guessed he could see all the way back down the river to the sea, if he found the right spot, so before he went inside he went looking for a path that would lead to the eastern edge.

He found a well-made path, gravelled and lined with stones the size of his fist. He followed the path under a magnif-icent bearded fig and came to a bench set under a tui tree.

He looked out at the horizon, squinting against the sun, and traced out the line of the river. There was that wall, some strange natural rampart it looked here, where the stone of the escarpment came curving across the landscape. There was the oddly heavy stretch of grassland, with glints of water through it so it looked more like a kind of reef-maze than a plain. There was the port where he had got off the sea train.

He couldn't see too far south, but he thought there might be a shadow on the horizon where those high islands had stood.

Then he looked up at the tui tree.

He had not seen one since he had left the Wide Seas; or more precisely, since he had passed that rough line beyond which the Islanders had never settled. There had been people living on Jilkano already when the ancestors sailed there, and on the coast along from Csiven. The ancestors had sailed there, traded a few items with the coastal peoples—most notably plants of sugar cane and bamboo for coffee and sweet potato—and turned back west.

East first, then west and home. That was the pattern in the *Lays*.

Islanders took tui trees with them, cuttings of the plants as they never set fruit, and planted them wherever they had settled. The only reason there would be a tui tree here was because Kip had brought it.

Tovo touched the bark, feeling the life of the tree, the sound of the breeze through its multitudes of fine leaflets familiar, friendly, after so many months hearing velioi sounds.

He turned back to look at the palace, which was visible rising up behind the bearded fig. If this was Kip's tree, as it must be, then somewhere on this side of the big stone building would be where he found Kip.

He followed the path back to a door, where a young man had just come out.

Tovo had never seen him before, but the young man stopped and stared at him in an astonishment that didn't seem the same as the stares Tovo had received for his clothing and accent his whole trip.

"I'm looking for Kip Mdang," he announced.

"I bet you are," the man muttered. He had a nice accent, not the mushy one Tovo had been hearing—which sounded as if everyone had a mouth full of that sticky sweet food that had stuck his teeth together—but with a sort of roundness to the vowels and sharpness to the consonants that had a nice effect. "Er—sir—are you—one of his relatives?"

Tovo appreciated a smart young man, especially one with such a nice body as this young man's was. Oh, it had been a long time since he'd last been tempted by a stranger, but he could still admire, couldn't he? He wasn't so old or blind that he couldn't see good muscles.

"His great-uncle," he declared. "Come to see what he's up to. Lots of people talking about him."

"I'm sure there are," the young man replied, his voice warming with amusement.

"You know him, eh?"

"I'm one of his Radiancy's guards—Pikabe is my name, sir," Pikabe said. "I went with them when they went to the Vangavaye-ve on holiday. I don't think I met you then, but you … have the look."

Tovo nodded, unsurprised. Tui trees were always good luck. For Islanders, anyway. "Did you go to Lesuia?"

"I did," Pikabe replied, and Tovo was interested to hear that wonder entered his voice. "The Moon came down."

Tovo shrugged away the Moon; from what Aya had told him that was all to do with the velioi poet-emperor or whatever he was. "There was a market, I heard," he said. "Anything happen there? With Kip?"

"At the market?" Pikabe hesitated, and then he said, "I was talking with some of the young women when they all stopped —everyone stopped—because Sayo, er, Lord Mdang—er, your Kip, that is, sir—was talking to an old man selling shells. One of the girls said, 'That's out of the *Lays*, that is,' the history-tales, and they made me listen."

"What did you see? What did you hear?"

Pikabe hesitated again. "I saw him hold up a length of shells, very beautiful shells, they looked like the sort of jewels his Radiancy wears, all gold and amber. I saw the old man look hard at him. I saw him, Lord Mdang, your Kip, stand as if he were—as if he were in a *story*."

"Mm," Tovo said, nodding.

"He said something about fire, I didn't understand but I could hear how his words rang in the air. Like a spear against a shield before a battle. It was a *challenge*. I think he was challenging the gods ... I told our shamans, in my village, when we got home. The Moon, she is not one of our gods, nor is whoever he was talking to, but if those gods are walking, then ..." Pikabe laughed a little nervously. "Then I thought maybe we shouldn't forget our own."

He was a guard, a warrior. Not an Islander thing, but still, a skill, learned and earned. Even though Kip had been speaking Islander, Pikabe had heard the challenge loud and clear: Tovo could trust that intuition, the same way he'd trust himself to know the winds had changed long before the storm came into sight.

"Do you need me to guide you?" Pikabe asked, looking down the path and then back at Tovo, his indecision clear.

"You've got a place to be, eh? Do I need you?"

"Seeing as you found your way here, I don't think you do! And yes, I do—look, sir, go down this hall to the end. There's an arched entry there, with a staircase—go up that, all the way up—five flights. You'll find Lord Mdang up there, or if not, people who will know where he is." Pikabe stepped back and opened the door for him.

"Thank you," Tovo said politely on entering, and stepped aside so the young man could head off in whatever tearing hurry he was in—young ones, always frantic, always rushing. Tovo wasn't rushing, no he wasn't.

Then again—he might have been going a little too slow, been a little too content to let himself keep his thoughts to himself unless someone came to ask him for them. That was not the only way to be tanà, that was for certain!

The hall was wide and cool, all pale stone and magic lights like glowing pearls. Tovo walked down, his feet pattering pleasantly on the cool floor. Fancy, fancy. There was art on the walls, sculptures on little stands here and there, pretty as could be.

Most of the hall was empty, but when he passed through the archway at the end there was a young woman in a pale brown dress. She was dark-skinned and elegant, holding her head up. Tovo nodded at her; she stared.

"What do you think you're doing?"

"I'm looking for Kip Mdang," he said, and went past her up the stairs.

"You—you can't go up there!"

"Was told to," he said imperturbably, to which she had no answer besides to follow along behind. She had a nice voice, all twittery like birds in a tree chattering about the morning. Tovo didn't understand a word she said once she got going, but it was no skin off his nose if she wanted to follow him.

Her noise attracted attention, of course, and as he rested on the first landing—he was ninety, he didn't climb stairs very often, he could stop to look at the large painting of a very fancy woman all dressed in shimmery ahalo cloth and heavy jewelry, black-skinned like he was told the emperors were.

There had been lots of stories about Kip's emperor, after that visit. The poet, Aya had said, describing a man Tovo could accept that his great-nephew could well want to follow.

Everyone *did* want to be Elonoa'a, that was the problem. Someone always went, across the horizon, one way or another. Some looked for new islands, some went to find old ones, some went to trade, and someone always went to see if this emperor was worth it.

Tovo started up again, ignoring the handful of new people in fancy clothes who had joined the first woman. None of their clothes were as fancy as the one in the painting, so he thought they probably weren't *that* important. Not if they were in a back stairway. This was not the way you went if you entered by the big fancy front doors, that was for sure.

Up, and up. And up. This was a great lot of stairs. Tovo couldn't imagine having to go down those every time you wanted to go outside. Yet Kip did, he must, to that tui tree he'd planted at the edge of the cliff, looking off to the east. East was not the right way—that was the *long* way home—but no doubt it was the sea that had called him. He might have to live away from the coast, away from the sound of the waves in his ears, the scent of the salt, but he could at least *look* on it every time he pleased.

Tovo had lost count of how many stairs he had climbed, but the staircase stopped so he decided that was probably the level he was supposed to reach. There was only one way to turn, so he turned that way, the whole jabbering mass of people who felt the need to follow him flooding out into the upper hall.

This was even fancier, or so he thought from fleeting glimpses between the velioi. There was a surge of voices rising in excitement, everyone talking over each other like a whole flock of seagulls fighting over fish guts, and then the space in front of him opened up.

There was a very fancy man in front of him. Tovo surveyed him swiftly, taking in the puffy bronze mushroom of a hat, the brilliant white tunic, the great sweep of ahalo cloth in a rich blue just the colour of the barnacle-beads on his own efela ko, the sandals all covered with jewels that glinted in the light.

Very fancy. He folded his arms, reminding himself that this was a velioi place, and Kip would have to follow velioi customs. He'd not come all this way not to listen to what Kip had to say as well as see what he could see.

His great-nephew stared at him in shock. "But you're dead!"

Tovo frowned sharply. Had no one heard he'd taken the sea train to go visit Kip?

Kip stared some more, his expression, if Tovo squinted, moving towards wonder. His voice was incredulous but increasingly full of joy. "Buru Tovo! You're alive!"

Was he just going to say stupid obvious things? And in that accent—following velioi customs or not was no excuse to mangle *his* name!

Tovo tutted to himself, cupped one hand around his ear—how often had he done that for the young Kip, who would talk and talk and talk and *talk* and forget to listen to any of the answers to his endless questions. "Eh what? Who's that? I'm looking for Kip Mdang!"

Kip smiled and walked forward. His silks and ahalo cloth rustled, like the wind in pandanus leaves, always a lovely sound. Tovo waited, easy as if he stood in front of his great-nephew's house, curious what greeting Kip would choose.

Kip placed his hands gently on Tovo's upper arms, the only part of the old imperial greeting anyone had ever liked—it was pretty much what the traditional greeting had involved, anyway—and looked deep in his face. This close Tovo could see Kip was obviously drinking in the sight of him, his eyes wide and full of emotion though his face was merely smiling slightly.

"Buru Tovo," Kip said, his accent already sharpening, so when he repeated Tovo's name the vowels sounded out properly. "Buru Tovo. It's Kip. I'm here."

Tovo peered at him, looking at the way Kip was looking at him. His great-nephew was ignoring all the twittering birdies. He grunted, and Kip smiled more genuinely, closing his eyes and then leaning forward to rest his forehead on Tovo's.

"There you are," Tovo said, leaning back and seeing with satisfaction that Kip's eyes and smile had sharpened, letting that fire catch. "Why were you wearing that? I didn't recognize you."

Kip's hands tightened on Tovo's arms, not unpleasantly but as if that had hit him a little too hard.

Well, he had to expect that, going away for so long and so

far and dressing like a velioi lord. Tovo jerked his head at the birdies. "Tell these people to go away. I need to talk to you."

~

The people left when Kip told them to, all of them bar two men with spears whom he thought had come with Kip from the other direction.

Tovo nodded to himself as Kip told one of them to take a message somewhere, no doubt wherever he'd been going. He made no comment to Tovo about that, though, turning around instead and guiding Tovo down the grand hallway and through some very fancy doors.

A Big Man's doorway, that was. Tovo hummed, looking at the men on either side of it, who were wearing matched clothing the same colours as Kip wore. That meant something, it did, and if Kip wore the colours too ... he nodded to himself, putting that in his mind to chew over as well. At home there were the Mdang patterns Kip might wear, or the tanà's if he claimed it in full, on a festival day.

Perhaps every day was a festival-day here, where you dressed in your finery to show off to everyone else. Tovo thought that might ruin the joy of a festival, which was partly the opportunity for the showing-off, but then, these were velioi, they liked to put things in rows all the time.

Through a room, another room, into one with chairs. Kip pointed him to one and sat down in the other. Tovo sat down, because he could see that Kip's clothes probably weren't suited for squatting, and he waited to see what his great-nephew would say.

"I thought you were dead, Buru Tovo. Would you like something to eat? To drink?"

Kip looked around as if he thought food and drink would

materialize out of thin air, which Tovo didn't think even the velioi did.

"Why would you think something that stupid?"

Kip said something about his age, and that everyone thought he'd gone to the Isle of the Ancestors, but Tovo was caught on the way Kip's accent was wavering, halfway between the sticky-mouthful and proper speech, and on the way his hands were gripping tight together, as if Kip could barely contain himself from reaching out to touch him.

That was a problem with these chairs. Hard to shift position quickly. Tovo sat back on his, bouncing a little on the seat. It was much softer than the chairs on the train or the boats. "I came on the train," he said, as someone came in and Kip waved the man back out.

"You came on the sea train?"

Maybe it was these velioi ways creeping in. Kip seemed much more bewildered than Tovo liked to see. Still, no sense rushing to a hasty judgement. Not after such a long journey. "That's what I said. Lots of people on it."

"What about when you got to Csiven?"

"That's the big city? Lots of people, eh." He nodded. "Found a wontok, they knew the way over the mountains. Lots of people talking about you, boy." He looked at his great-nephew, who was intent on every word. What a way to be a tanà!

It had taken him a long time, but Kip had eventually learned the value of listening first. Looking first, there he'd always been clever, seeing what was truly there. But the third part of being a good tanà, asking the right question at the right time ... oh, that had always been hard for him.

"But why did you come? Just to see me?"

Still was, seemed like.

Tovo snorted. "Lots of people talking about you, boy."

"At home? Along the way?"

A question, but not a very good question, was it? Tovo considered even as the man from before came in with a tray of some sort of refreshments. Kip waved at him and the man looked a little surprised before disappearing again.

Hmm, Tovo thought. That was a Big Man's way, having someone else bring the hospitality.

Kip offered him a bowl of water, cupped between his hands in what was probably a velioi custom. Tovo narrowed his eyes at him. "What's this for?"

"Washing your hands," Kip replied, glancing down at the water.

"Washed them already, down in the yard."

Not that Tovo wouldn't mind washing them again, of course, he'd gone all around the gardens since then, patted the tui tree and so on, but that wasn't quite the point.

"It's the custom here, Buru."

Kip and Aya, they were about the only two who called him *Buru* at all times. Aya because she loved the *Lays* and wanted to live in their pattern. Kip—well! He *had* wanted to live in their pattern. The question was: did he still?

And *that* was a question whose time had come to be asked. Tovo looked straight at his great-nephew. "You keep any of the old ways, boy? I didn't come all this way to see you a fancy-man and foreign."

Kip paused, and Tovo could see the answer cross his face, bright as a viau across the sky.

Oh, but Kip had never liked to claim what was too true, had he? He'd shout all his thoughts about everything you should be doing, but he held his own heart close as a single ember.

"Why did you come?" Kip asked, one hand shifting to the old, old gesture that meant *I am listening to you*, which Tovo did not think he'd done at all on purpose.

That was not too bad, not too bad at all.

Tovo laughed, the relief in him almost a kookaburra-cackle like his own god. "Wanted to see the world before I go to the ancestors," he said. "Wanted to see you again before. Wanted—"

But Kip, never quite right on the timing of his questions, not when it was closest to his heart, jumped in: "Yes?" And then, a moment later, he flushed and looked down, his hands up in apology, just as he had any hundred times when he was a boy. "No! I remember. Listen first. Questions later."

Tovo felt his inner judgment tilting ever so slowly over to *yes*. But—oh, he knew better than to judge too hastily, didn't he? For something as important as this? He could not judge according to his own desire—or even according to Kip's. The surface winds might blow the way of the current, but then again they might not.

"Haven't forgotten everything, then," he muttered, and waved Kip off back to whatever velioi things he felt he had to do.

The man who had come in before was named Franzel, and he showed Tovo through the rooms until they unexpectedly arrived at a bedroom.

"And do you have any clothes that need ... cleaning?" the man asked.

Tovo considered, and pulled out the poncho. "This probably does. How often do you velioi wash things?"

Franzel had a small twitch in his cheek, it turned out. Tovo thought back to what everyone else had done on the train and barge, and guessed maybe it was about the washing.

"When they're dirty," Franzel said, his voice admirably calm.

Tovo nodded. "Different than ours. It needs to be brushed

out from time to time," he said, gesturing at his grass skirt. "And of course you need to tend it. Tie in new leaves, fix the beading, that sort of thing."

Franzel's cheek twitched again, but curiosity was competing against horror in his eyes. "How old is your skirt ... sir?"

Tovo fingered the fringe of his skirt. "How old? I made it when I was, oh, younger than Kip." He grinned at the man. "Then again, is it the same skirt when all the parts have been replaced a hundred times?"

Franzel hesitated, then he reached slowly for the poncho. "I'll take this, then, sir."

"Tanà, if you need a title. Velioi always like titles, I've found. That's mine."

Franzel looked down at his efela, which was a very pleasing response and suggested that Kip was doing something right.

Tovo touched his efetana. "This one, that's right. Efetana. Fire coral."

"Lord Mdang doesn't have that one," Franzel said, with the barest hint of a question.

"No," Tovo agreed equably. "Maybe one day. Maybe not. We'll see."

Franzel nodded, then spent a few minutes briskly showing Tovo the various features of the room, which included a very fancy bath Tovo eyed with great interest, and what turned out to be a bed and not a tent, and then left him to himself.

Tovo figured Kip was a busy busy man in the velioi way, to be draped with all that ahalo cloth and silk, and so had a bath.

Clean, his skirt brushed out and tended, Tovo wandered through the rooms opening off his. He soon discovered there was some sort of patterning with the surrounds of the doors, though it took him a few tries to work out that the sun went not east-to-west but rather in-to-out, and the moon signs the opposite. The other pictures were pretty enough but he didn't bother to memorize any of them.

It was obvious that Kip himself only used a few of the rooms. Tovo found his bedroom, which was pretty much the same as the one he'd been given except that Kip had a stack of books beside his bed and a couple of very nice hangings from home on the wall.

Good enough. Tovo poked through the gorgeous costumes in the room that was given over to them. Towards the back of one of the closets was a carefully hung grass skirt. Tovo touched it, recognizing the pattern and the knots.

So. Kip never had learned any other way of tying skirts besides the one he had learned from Tovo himself.

And he had one.

Something to think about, that was for sure.

There was always lots to think about, with Kip.

He went out to find a room where Kip clearly spent much of his time, and in which there was a large painting Tovo was rather surprised to recognize.

Long, long ago, when he was young, Tovo had sailed first east and then west to see what he could see.

Well. There had been more to it than that.

But call it that, yes.

He looked at the painting, which was the one that velioi artist had done of him, when Tovo had come across the prince-heir of the Empire on some sort of festival progress. They'd been on barges, barely seaworthy to Tovo's eyes; they hadn't dared go out of sight of land.

What a strange person Kip was. Full of velioi ways, but with a picture of Tovo on the wall of his hearth-room, as if to be his anchor.

A Mdang through and through, with that streak of the contrary to him.

Tovo had told his niece to be careful what she told her son he couldn't do.

~

Kip came back in his fancy clothes and the perfumes that were not the flowers people wore on the islands. He greeted Tovo with all the formalities he'd already performed and a few more that might or might not be the velioi ways.

None of this told Tovo what he'd come to find out, but it was not yet time for those questions. He looked his great-nephew up and down, taking in the confident posture, the subtle power and authority in his angle of his chin and the look in his eyes.

Oh, Kip had learned some of his lessons well. Tovo saw so much of himself in Kip it almost hurt to look at him and doubt.

"Very fancy," he said.

"It's the custom here," Kip replied, his voice suddenly wavering, uncertain, thirteen.

"Bah. Sit."

Just as he had when he was thirteen, Kip sat.

With some effort, Tovo did not roll his eyes. He'd had enough of chairs, and squatted down beside him instead, looking up at his great-nephew. Kip looked rather like a chief on a platform.

After a moment Kip slid down, his fancy clothes slithering down beside him, and sat cross-legged on the floor, again as if he were thirteen and sitting at Tovo's feet.

Tovo grunted thoughtfully. This was interesting.

He squatted there, Kip sitting at his feet and gazing quietly up at him, just as he had when he was past the choppy waters of his earliest apprenticeship and had started to learn the patience and calm that one needed if one were to learn the *Lays* properly.

Kip was full of contradictions. Very fancy—*very* fancy—standing proud and certain in all the velioi ways, wearing ahalo cloth and all the finery of a great chief. And yet—

He had a proper Islander skirt in amongst all his other clothes. He had that picture of the young Tovo. He sat quietly at Tovo's feet, waiting for ... something.

Franzel came in with a tray, looked aghast to see them sitting on the floor, set the tray down, and left again. Kip looked at the items, some sort of flower-fragrant hot drink, but didn't move either to take them or offer them to Tovo. He simply ... waited.

Tovo sat there, thinking of what Aya had told him of the market-day. How Kip had looked fancy, a city man, not wearing finery; and how when the efelauni had asked him the questions out of the *Lays*, Kip had stepped forward without hesitation and put himself right into them.

The tanà of the world outside the Ring, Aya had called him, standing beside the fire at the centre of the palace.

But not the tanà at home. Not yet. Kip had left, as someone always left, to see what lay on the other side of the horizon, to find his heart's desire, to get fire from the house of the sun. To see if *this* emperor was worth sailing to find.

They came home, the sons of Vonou'a. Elonoa'a had come home, too, before he left again to follow his emperor.

Kip had come home, and gone again, and stayed away.

Tovo had been on Loaloa when Kip had come home after his first long time away. There had been too many deaths that year, and he'd been needed at home, though his sister, Kip's grandmother, died in the city. Tovo had not seen Kip until after he'd already decided to leave again, and by then the boy—young man—was brittle and sharp as a sliver of obsidian, all his words turned out, as if he'd never learned a thing from Tovo.

And yet ...

Tovo was old, and sometimes it was easier to remember the distant past than the more recent. He could see that Kip in his mind's eye: the way he stood firmly planted on the boardwalks of Gorjo City, feet angled as if to dance. The expression on his face, defiant and hurting and looking for something he'd been unable to find at home.

Had he found it here?

There were questions Tovo had never asked him. He could admit he should have, seeing Kip in that state, but he'd been deep in his own grief, and Kip's rejection of home had been hard to bear. Tovo hadn't shouted at him, hadn't wept over his decision, but he had probably ... oh, certainly ... been ... disappointed.

He had truly thought Kip would be the one to follow him, to be tanà; to be tana-tai. Had been *proud* of his brilliance, his wit, his courage, his stubbornness, that contrary streak of the Mdangs married to the fearlessness and fortitude of his father's family, the Vargas.

He hadn't liked the evidence that he was wrong. And maybe he'd shown that.

Tovo considered the memory, dwelled in that brief conversation they'd had outside Lazo's place. Tovo had been busy, trying to hold together too many griefs, too many deaths, and Kip had—

What *had* Kip said?

Tovo had been in a rush, he remembered that. He had regretted the rush, later. It had taken him a long time to repair some of the things that had broken in that period.

It had never really occurred to him that Kip was one of them.

Kip had always been Kip, sharp-tongued and sharp-witted

and determined and so, so brilliant. Tovo had not been at all surprised when Kip left. It was always the brilliant ones who needed to see the outside world first before they could find it in them to love the Ring.

Tovo had been in a rush. Kip had been outside Lazo's place, not going in, *refusing* to go in, but yet hanging around outside. He'd called out to Tovo, who had of course stopped, because he hadn't seen Kip in, oh, seven years, eight years, not since before he'd left.

Stopped, but he'd been in a rush, and Kip had been uncharacteristically slow to start talking, and Tovo had said something about how he didn't have time, he had to go—

And he had had to go, there had been a ceremony that had to be done at a certain time, part of the mourning rites. There were a few things the tana-tai did, when a matriarch of a family died.

Kip had known that. He'd *known* that Kip had known that. He'd *taught* him that.

Kip had nodded, and stepped back, and said nothing more than that it was good to see him.

Tovo had gone off to the ceremony, content in the knowledge that Kip would find him if it was important, would tell him whatever it was when there was time.

And since then ... well, Kip hadn't come to find him. Tovo had maybe thought about looking for him once or twice, but there *had* been a lot of deaths that year, and Kip was not ready for those sorts of responsibilities, had not tried to take them upon his shoulders.

Had, instead, quietly left again on the velioi ship, and though he had come home to visit, he had never again come to stay.

He'd never claimed the dances, never claimed efetana, never asked Tovo the questions that would lead to either.

And Tovo had thought perhaps he'd been wrong, that Kip

had been like any of the other dozens of people who had sat at his feet for a season or two, learning the fire, learning the *Lays*, but who had not been see how to step into the *Lays*, to live them, let alone to challenge them.

But he had wondered, when Kip still called him *Buru*, and because it was his place to hold the fire, he had held that small ember of possibility that Kip had not forgotten all the steps.

That the old traditions did not stop with Tovo, because no one was willing to come after him. You could not *make* someone hold the fire; they would only burn.

According to Aya, Kip had stood before Vou'a and promised a new fire for the hearth of the world.

He turned his head to his great-nephew, whose face was quiet, thoughtful. The bells rang again, which Tovo would have found intolerable but Kip ignored.

According to those of the family who had come to visit him here, Kip had become a fancy-man and foreign, and claimed no status beyond what he did at home, which was negligible. Far from being the shining star who showed them a new island, a new fire, a new way, he kept himself firmly in the place he'd had when he'd *left*.

Tovo turned that thought in his mind.

People talked as if Kip was a bit of a disappointment.

No. People talked as if *other people* thought Kip was a bit of a disappointment. People on Loaloa talked about how he was too fancy, too citified, too foreign, too successful *outside the Ring*, too much of a Big Man, to remember them. *They* all asked after him, every time. Every time.

Tovo was forever saying, "Someone always leaves. He'll come back when it's time."

And what had *he* meant? All this past year, walking the Ring?

Did he think that Kip would come back from his years

away and slip into Tovo's place without a change, without a ripple?

That was not what it meant to be tana-tai! That was *why* the tana-tai was the one who went to get a striking rock from the far side of the horizon: because the fire was made with one tovo from the Ring and one tanaea from away. That was how you made a *new* fire.

The people did not need another Tovo. They did not need another Lazo, excellent as he was as tanà in the city. They needed—

Tovo looked again at his great-nephew. They needed someone who could sit quietly in all his velioi finery, through all the bells that called summonses, proud enough to lift his chin before the Son of Laughter and step immediately into the *Lays* when he was asked the right questions, humble enough to sit at the feet of his elder.

They needed Kip.

"Not so bad, boy," Tovo said roughly. "Thought you might have lost all the quiet here. Good enough."

He sprang up, laughing when Kip moved more slowly and stiffly, because—oh, a velioi Big Man did not sit on the floor like that, that Franzel's face had said as much. "Need to move more, boy, or you'll be old before your time."

"I'm afraid you're right, Buru."

He grunted. "Got that right." An odd note there in Kip's voice, in his eye. There had been some strange comments about time and the palace folk. Well, never mind that. "You want to know why I came, eh?"

"Yes, please, Buru."

So had the young Kip spoken every time!

Well, not *every* time. Sometimes he'd shouted. Kip had not been very measured, not when he was first given over to Tovo's company when his mother was in total despair over the boy.

("He's so smart," she'd wailed to him. "But he won't

listen!" Tovo could have told his niece of, oh, a dozen Mdangs of the same sort, including herself, but he'd simply said he'd see what he could do.)

"Lots of people talking about you," he said, nodding. "Lots of people. Thought it about time someone saw what it was all about."

"Mama and some of the others came to visit."

Kip's tone was about as neutral as it could be, which Tovo didn't blame him for, no not at all. Eidora was a lovely woman but she had never quite understood her son. Too similar, maybe, in temperament. Stubborn, the whole lot of them. Never admitting they were wrong.

Tovo snorted. "They came to see what they were looking for. Too close. Even that Quintus cousin of yours. He's a chief at heart, that one. Big ship, big man. He might dance Aōtētana, but he knows he'll never dance Aōteketētana. Not got the mind to hold the fire."

Oh, if he hadn't heard that story from Aya he might not have said that, and then he would have missed the way Kip's heart suddenly shone bright as the sunrise in his face.

"Buru, did you—"

Kip stopped himself, hard, visibly making his face go calm.

Tovo laughed. "Not so fancy to have forgotten everything, eh?"

"No, Buru."

That was very soft. Not the proud stepping into the *Lays.* "Speak up, boy." Kip looked down, just as if he were that young apprentice being told to stop asking questions and *listen.* Which ... was the beginning, not the end. At some point the tanà had to ask the questions.

Tovo couldn't remember ever once telling Kip to *ask* a question. It had always been a matter of getting him to stop long enough to listen to the answer, to use his own mind, to form his own judgments.

And so he stood here, in that velioi finery, tanà of the world.

"You've been a long time from home, boy."

"Yes, Buru."

There was no hesitation, no pretence there. Tovo thought back again to that moment outside Lazo's place, that time Kip first came home after his long journey. Tovo had made a mistake there, not listened when someone couldn't quite find the words to ask the question they needed to ask.

The tanà, confronted with a fire, tended it.

The tana-tai, given a tangle of threads, sorted them out.

"Missed a lot of the ceremonies," Tovo said, following one of the threads. "Barely know your island."

Kip did not protest that harsh judgment. He looked down. "Yes, Buru."

So. Kip was still sitting at his feet, was he? Or—wanted to.

No. He had seen that viau flash across Kip's face. Kip wanted to dance the fire for him. Wanted it so badly he could not utter even the hint of it.

Tovo might have missed this, if he hadn't held that small ember of hope that Kip had not forgotten everything he'd taught him, if he hadn't been willing to hear Aya when she told him of the *Lays* coming suddenly real in that moment when Kip picked up a strand of shells from the efelauni who was the god of mysteries.

He considered how best to do this, to show Kip that Tovo had held that ember, and it was time to fan it to a flame. Kip was a proud, stubborn man. He needed to feel this was *real*.

And it could not wait. Tovo could not wait, not with this tangle dropped in his lap. He couldn't say it was the wrong time of year or the wrong place or the wrong situation. This was the place they were, the time they were, the situation the gods had given him to work with.

"In the old days, the days of the voyages," he said slowly,

thinking his way to the right words, "they did the ceremonies at the right time. Didn't worry so much about the right place."

Kip looked up at him, face set but his eyes full of that sunrise-light. Tovo looked at the thoughts passing like birds in his eyes, and wished he had told Kip he'd never given up on seeing his sail come home.

Another bell tolled, deep and longer than the others. Tovo guessed it was sunset, or something like that. Perhaps something else velioi needed to mark. But did Kip?

"No sun, no stars. Need the bells to show the way, do you?"

That was the thing about the tana-tai, or anyone who talked with the gods. It was challenge after challenge; the *Lays* were full of them.

Kip smiled, and Tovo saw then exactly what Aya had seen.

"I came to sit at the feet of the Sun, Buru."

Tovo could only laugh at his own folly at never asking the questions of Kip because he had been afraid of what he might answer. "Do you? You want the fire, do you?"

"Yes."

"Then bring me the sun and the stars, boy, to witness your life and see if it is worthy of the fire."

4

If someone—Kip, for instance—had challenged Tovo like that, he would have shown them his striking rock, his efetana and his efela ko, and the kookaburra feathers in his hair.

The first for the long journeys he had taken to understand the *Lays* as they were and as they might be now; the two efela to show his anchor of home and his vocation as tanà; and the feathers to show his quiet, private relationship with the Son of Laughter.

Kip went off, leaving Tovo to talk with Franzel about proper food, none of this fancy foreign stuff, and came back with his emperor and velioi friends.

Tovo considered this a quite remarkable choice, and amused himself while they waited for the velioi to show up by needling Kip about the furniture. He did accept that a velioi Big Man—and the emperor was, even he could admit, a very Big Man—would not be happy about sitting on the floor.

The first one to come in was a fine figure of a man. Tovo inspected him thoroughly.

All these fine figures of men! It was a pity Kip had never

shown much interest, in either men *or* women for that matter. Tovo had always wondered what Kip's once-girlfriend Ghilly had thought she was about, and been glad for her sake she'd married that Toucan fellow instead.

But yes: a fine figure of a man, all muscles and rich brown skin, his hair a little short and his eyes a little melancholy. Oh, if only Tovo were fifty years younger! He could have put a smile on that stolid face. The man had long golden marks down his arms and hands, very curious. Not like Tanaea's vitiligo, or at least Tovo didn't think so.

Regardless, this man didn't seem to be quite the same sort of velioi as the rich ones. Tovo asked the ritual questions, then, seeking where to put him. "What is your name, what is your island, what is your dance?"

The man lifted one hand up, in a sharp formal gesture. "My name is Ludvic Omo. My island is Woodlark in the Azilint. We do not have your dances, but the head of my carving is Odongai."

No hesitation, and a glimmer of amusement in those sad eyes. A fine man indeed. If he were fifty years younger! "Ey ana. What are your markings, there?"

"They are scars from my service."

"That's how you do it, boy," Tovo said to Kip, who was hovering impatiently (Tovo could have told him that no one ever rushed the sun and the stars, and if he chose people for those positions he'd have to let them have their own rhythms or he'd be sore regretful), and turned his attention onto Ludvic, who turned out to have a slow humour about him Tovo very much liked.

~

Kip's emperor had odd eyes.

Tovo watched him coming in, the velioi Big Man in his fancy, fancy clothes, and watched Kip's response.

Kip's glance darted behind the Big Man, looking for—attendants, maybe. Guards. Big Men were usually attended by their nephews or sons, their advisors and sometimes their friends. Tovo didn't think that a velioi Big Man would be any different, maybe in the particulars but not in the general idea.

So for this one to come in without those expected attendants, with the other men apparently Kip's friends, was a good thing.

He had done it on purpose, his words in answer to Kip's silent question clear and clear.

Tovo noted that Kip's emperor knew Kip well enough to answer his silent questions. That Kip would watch and listen and respond to *his* in return, well, that was the sort of thing one would expect, for someone who wanted to be as Elonoa'a to his Emperor. Kip might have his moments of impatience and obtuseness, but he *was* good at seeing to the heart, when he looked.

Big Men did not usually look with such attention and care —love, one might say—on those below them.

The tanà stood beside, not below, of course, but that was an Islander way, and the velioi might be different.

But if different, then that suggested that Kip had taught his emperor well.

Kip did some sort of fancy velioi bow and then doubled it with the Islander courtesy before gathering his words together. "My lord, may I present my great-uncle, Buru Tovo inDaina of Loala? Buru Tovo, the Sun-on-Earth."

Tovo flicked his eyebrows at his great-nephew—what sort of introduction was *that*?—but what a title! no wonder Kip had been half-inclined to follow this man from the first moment he saw him.

He bowed over his hands when Kip's emperor gravely

inclined his head. Tovo regarded him intently. It was the Islander way to challenge, to push, to see what a person or a people were made of.

Time to see what Kip's emperor was made of.

"I met your uncle once, when he was a young man," he said. Kip's emperor went quite oddly still, a flash running through his eyes, but he met Tovo's, smiling slightly and his odd yellow eyes catching a shimmer, like a breaking wave showing a hidden reef.

Well, well, well.

"You don't look much like him," Tovo went on, watching as a kind of relief crested in the man's eyes.

Relief: that was odd. No one should *want* to be much like what's-his-name the last emperor.

Had this emperor thought himself too similar? He would only know the *Lays* from Kip's teaching of them, but he would have his own stories and patterns to follow. Perhaps being emperor was a rip tide he was not sure he had escaped.

Most of what's-his-name problems had come from inside, but there were plenty that came from the position. All Big Men were in danger of getting too swollen a head, after all, especially one who'd been born to it, not chosen.

Tovo tipped his head at Kip's emperor. "What should I call you, then?"

A second test, or maybe third—he was getting old, but the number of them didn't matter. Just that each test was offered, met, and from the response one either pushed harder or stepped back, having reached a limit. Some limits were meant to be stepped over, others to be held firm.

Kip's emperor wanted to give him a different one, Tovo could see it in his eyes, but he said, "Lord Artorin," just as if that was his name.

Velioi.

Tovo looked at Kip's other friends, presumably the stars if

the Sun-on-Earth (*what* a title) was his sun, and Kip introduced them to him with all their long sonorous names and titles. They looked at him, surprised, as if Kip had made some strange misstep in velioi customs. Kip clearly knew what they were looking like that for but just lifted his chin.

"So, boy," Tovo said, taking minor pity on his great-nephew's discombobulation (Tanaea was right, that word *did* have a nice sound to it), "do we eat now, or talk first? It's your house."

Kip's expression suggested he'd never thought of it that way. He said something about the custom of eating after sunset.

"Bah, talk first, then," Tovo said, watching how Kip's emperor's eyes softened as he looked at Kip's confusion. "Sit down, Lord Artorin, I can't think where that boy's manners have gone. He used to know better."

"He is torn between two cultures, I think."

That showed a fair grasp of Kip's behaviour, at least. Kip flinched a little when Tovo called him *Lord Artorin*, whereas his emperor had a strangely opaque look in his eyes. Definitely had another name he'd prefer but didn't want to say out loud —probably the rebel poet or whatever Aya had mentioned.

"Relax, boy, you look like you're waiting for a storm to hit. Lord Artorin—" There was that minuscule flinch again. Velioi! "My boy there wants me to tell him he can claim the fire. Trying not to look as if he already has."

The emperor laughed like a real person, eyes scrunching up and all. Kip looked down, flushing and smiling in a way that said he was pleased at the laughter, embarrassed at the truth of Tovo's comment, and ready to claim the fire in truth. Tovo relaxed another smidgen. If Kip's emperor could laugh with joy and good humour... well, there wasn't too much wrong with a Big Man who could laugh, especially if he could laugh at himself. Though that still stood in question.

Kip's emperor was a poet, Tovo reminded himself. A secret poet, even, who had been some sort of criminal before he inherited his title. He had a way of seeing to the heart of things, too. He looked at Tovo, solemn but not serious, and asked: "What does he need to do to prove his worthiness to you? He said something about the sun and the stars?"

"Ey ana, that's the way of it." Tovo grinned at his great-nephew's embarrassment. Kip's ability to avoid explaining what he was feeling never ceased to exasperate. "He'll tell us the way of his life by the signs he has used to direct it. Come, boy, get yourself ready already."

Kip did not mind being called *boy*, not the way his emperor minded *Lord Artorin*.

Mind you, it was probably nice, in its way, to have an elder to look to for guidance. It was easy to forget, sitting here in Kip's cozy hearth-room as Kip moved a metal brazier to the centre and lit a fire in it, that both Kip and his emperor were very Big Men, and had the weight of the world on their shoulders.

Oh, Tovo knew the weight of being tana-tai, and how it was a gift to be able to meet someone like Kuaso as a peer. Not that there wouldn't be a challenge there, of course, any more than Tovo wouldn't challenge Kip now, but still. Tovo looked forward to the day, if he lived to see it, when *he* went to Kip for advice.

Tovo watched Kip light the fire in the velioi way, which had the merit of taking bare seconds. When the fire had caught —first try, of course it was first try—he said, "So, boy, when was the last time you danced any part of the Fire?"

Tovo did not hold his breath. He had been waiting for the answer half his life. One day—

Kip lifted his chin and spoke as solidly as he must have spoken to Vou'a. "This morning."

—One day the answer would be the one he longed to hear.

Tovo couldn't answer directly, not at first. He made a little time to recover by noticing the velioi were confused, so he asked Kip to expand a little, explain.

"Each family has its dances," Kip said. "Ours, mine, are *Aōtetana,* or properly ... *Aōteketētana*—the dances of Those Who Hold the Fire. I practice ... I have a practice room, I have mats on the floor, I have drawn the patterns, Buru Tovo, and I dance them."

Tovo listened, noting that Kip was not exactly explaining the full depth of meaning and skill involved in the dances.

Far too close to his heart, no doubt. One day Kip would realize that the way to keep a single ember safe was to light a fire with it.

"So you haven't forgotten all the steps. What of the rest? What is your wealth?"

Tovo did not like the Shaian word, but it was clear Kip's friends would not get the full extent of what efela meant. Well, they would see what *wealth* meant by what Kip showed them.

Kip got up, went over to a boxy piece of furniture over by the wall, under the painting, and pulled out a basket from inside.

The basket wasn't in a traditional style, but the efela were. The first one, the most recent—or at least the last one Kip had put in the basket—was the long strand of efevoa.

Tovo wore the kookaburra feathers, which he'd been given by Vou'a. He did not himself have efevoa, but then again his promise had been more personal, more private. A secret, for the god of secrets, not answer to a challenge.

He looked at Kip's efela. There must be nearly fifty sundrop cowries. Fifty! The Son of Laughter must have laughed hard to hear Kip speak forth such a promise as that.

He looked at the other men. They had maybe seen the shells before, if they'd all been at that market, but not close-to.

The efevoa were very near the colour of Kip's emperor's eyes, all amber and gold.

"Tell us the story of their coming to you," Tovo said.

Kip told the story Aya had, albeit summarizing more, in that dismissive way he had when he was very, very proud of something. Tovo had always thought it an odd quirk for a boy so adamantly expressive, but then again Kip had always been pushed to do better and not to boast.

Tovo wanted to shake him. Winning a fifty-shell strand of efevoa from the god of mysteries was *precisely* what one should boast of.

Kip said his promise with such utmost earnestness that Tovo could only laugh, the same way his god had laughed, for no one but Kip—in all the Ring, no one but Kip—could possibly have said he would bring a new fire to the hearth of the world and mean it literally.

Kip had always wanted to be Elonoa'a or the third son of Vonou'a: to follow an emperor worth following, and to bring home fire.

Well. He had followed his emperor. Who was Tovo to say he would not also bring home a new fire?

"What did he say, your efelauni?"

Kip cocked his head at the word. But he smiled crookedly at Tovo. "He laughed at me like a kookaburra and said to be sure I did."

"You meet the Son of Laughter and tell him you're bringing a new fire to the Islands, you'd better believe he'll be watching," Tovo replied, part warning and part promise. Kip's eyes were wide, that sunrise-light flooding into it. Tovo forced himself not to roll his eyes, something he never had to do so much as with Kip. What had his great-nephew *thought* that had meant? "What else have you go in there, boy?"

Nothing, Tovo thought, could possibly be as astonishing as the efevoa.

But he was wrong, as he had been wrong more than once with Kip, for at the bottom of the basket, under a lifetime of efela that showed the gradual accumulation of knowledge, of confidence, of experience, of wealth, there was the spiral shell of Ani's Tear.

Tovo was not too proud to admit he stared at that shell for a long, long moment before he could speak.

He'd seen Ani's Tear once before, when he was quite a young man himself. There had been an old woman of Looenna, a great healer, who had sailed in her youth to see if the emperor of those days was worth following. She had left, and returned, and on her way home had studied with the lore-keepers of a dozen archipelagos that had not yet lost their knowledge.

She had found the last new island in Tovo's memory, the eerily beautiful raised atoll of Aōreloke'ea, the Dance of Hidden Stars, whose coral mountains held hidden lakes filled with silver-glowing jellyfish. She had been given the gift of Ani's Tear for that finding, for the sea had loved it when the Islanders found new islands.

Kip held the spiral shell, blue as the sea, in his cupped hands.

"Ey ana," Tovo said finally, when his voice would sound. "Efani. How did you come by that?"

And Kip, who had always, always kept his heart close as a single ember in a fire-pot, looked down at the shell, and up at first his emperor, and then at Tovo, and finally said, "It's a long story of the sea to tell it."

Tovo barely stopped himself from crying out in joy and relief, for after all, after all, Kip had not forgotten everything.

Not forgotten *anything*.

Tovo was the tana-tai. He had heard many secrets before, and he knew when it was time to ask questions, and how to show his ears were open to hear what was answered. "We sit by the fire ready to hear it."

And what a long tale of the sea it was.

~

Kip sketched out the collapse of the empire in such bare outlines Tovo could hear the pain the memory still held for him. All the news of the Wide Seas he had heard, Kip said—over and again Kip said it—was that across the Wide Seas there was *a wall of storms*.

Back home they had seen the wall of storms, but it had been long and long since any Islanders had gone looking for new islands, and the trade-ships that came were mostly Shaian ones. When the wall of storms raised up against the sky and did not dissipate, and the trade-ships stopped coming, people muttered of the wrath of Ani and prayed more than they had before to the old gods of the Ring.

Tovo had been home when the earthquake rumbled through the Ring: an earthquake that shook reality, not the earth. There had been no great waves, tsunamis or seiches, outside or inside the Ring. But there had been an endless singular moment when it felt as if all things were falling apart. And then there had been the storms.

Kip spoke of sending letters that went nowhere. He spoke of drowning his grief and pain in work, of trying to rebuild what had shattered. Tovo listened to the things he did not say, watching the way Kip's hands clenched and twisted, the way his friends kept their faces carefully blank, though their eyes were full of their own dark memories.

Kip did not say he had lit a fire, but Tovo was tanà and tana-tai, and he knew what it took to hold a community together.

Kip spoke of an admiral, some ship's commander, who

decided to sail to the Vangavaye-ve to find her family, and how he did not go himself.

"I should have gone," Kip said, his voice low and broken. "As soon as I saw the ship go I knew I should have gone. I didn't go. I let her go without me. I did not stand up for what I knew was the right decision."

Tovo wondered what Kip was not saying. He had never been weak. If he had not gone to follow his heart's desire, and he was already in the strange and unknown new land, then he stayed because there was a fire to tend or his emperor to stand beside. It did not seem as if he had been standing beside his emperor, not then, and therefore it was a fire.

The tanà held the fire. They held the embers and lit new fires when the time came. The fire was the literal fire, of course —in the old, old days of the voyagers it had been a fine and necessary wisdom, the knowledge of how to keep a fire through all those long journeys—but it was, even more, the lore and the *Lays* that held a community together and told the people who they were.

There was no shame, Tovo thought, in Kip having decided to tend the fire he held until it was strong enough to burn in others' care. That he sat where he was now, so many years on, was proof enough he had done so.

Kip's emperor said something about the chief Kip had counselled in those days, which was maybe part of it, but Kip had never been one to truckle to authority. He was too contrary for that. He would sit at Tovo's feet, but it had taken him a long, long time to be willing to listen.

"I was weak," Kip said. "I should have gone."

Tovo watched him press his hands across the fabric of his clothes. This was a wound that had never quite healed, then. "You didn't," he said simply. "What did you do?"

Kip had worked until the fire was strong, waiting for word to come that never came. And then—he had set out.

Kip had walked across those grey, stony mountains. He had been chased across those high, precarious rope bridges. He had begged and traded words for food. He had convinced people to carry him across the near seas, between the shore where that big city was now—Csiven, that's right—and one island, another island, Jilkano where those hopping creatures were.

Kip walked across the middle of that great island, the mountains and the desert, and persuaded someone to sail him to Nijan, and there he found a wontok.

And that wontok, a Nga from Lobau in the Isolates, had taught Kip to make a boat.

That surprised him. "You made a boat? The old way?"

"Yes. At the time I did think how much you would approve—and how much I already knew how to do, once I was reminded, thanks to your teaching."

Kip went on, describing the skills he had learned, relearned, and Tovo sat back, listening as Kip's emperor skillfully pulled out a thread of humour, a moment of connection, bringing Kip back from too deep in his memories.

It was good, Tovo thought, that Kip had found such a friend. That was what the *Lays* always said of Elonoa'a and his emperor, that they were the greatest of *friends*. Great enough for Elonoa'a to have sailed out of the world to go looking for his friend when he went missing.

Looking at the two of them, the way Kip looked at his emperor and his emperor looked at Kip, Tovo could see that this was a friendship maybe as deep as that.

When the boat was built, Kip's teacher had gone with him, saying he could carry the fire and she would read the wind.

But she had not survived the great storms, and Kip had sailed alone across the Wide Seas in a boat of his own hands' building, dancing the fire over and over again until he knew it with every fibre of his being and was able, in the end, to be in such harmony with the ancestors and the Wide Seas that the fire dance showed him the way home.

Tovo knew that the dances held that teaching, but even by his day he had only been able to match a handful of islands to the steps.

Cast off his ke'ea by every storm, in his tiny boat he had to rebuild on every island, Kip had recovered that ancient knowledge.

"And when I danced I remembered you told me that this was our store of knowledge. Is it permitted, Buru, to speak of these things before velioi?"

"They are the sun and the stars of your witnessing, boy."

Which Tovo still did not quite understand, except that somehow his emperor held him to his course, and his friends helped him shape the boat he sailed on it.

"You had told me that the dances showed the way, that the fire dance was the record of our family's journeys, all that had been done in the old days when we crossed the Wide Seas."

All that had been done.

Tovo's great-uncle, who had taught him the ways, had told him all the deepest secrets he knew, and said, sorrowfully, that there were more that had been lost over time. To Tovo the fire dance was the pattern of the *Lays*, the shape of the Islands, the guide and warning and challenge of what it was to be tanà. It was not a *map*.

Maps, he had always thought, were a velioi idea.

Maps, maybe: but not the idea of tracing out ke'ea in song and dance, passing it on to those who came after, showing them the way.

Tovo listened to Kip describing his journey, how he had fallen ever deeper into the study of the *Lays*, the fire dance, until he *knew* that dance the way no one, perhaps, had since the days of Tupaia, who had been the tanà who stood beside

Elonoa'a and sailed off with him to search Sky Ocean for their emperor.

And Tovo had thought, they all had thought, that Kip had turned his back on the Ring and left this all behind.

Island to island, all those scattered atolls and high mountains who were barely names in the long catalogues of the *Lays*. Tovo had taught those to the young Kip, when Kip had finished making his efela ko and sailed each year back and forth across the Bay of the Waters, seeking the way to being tanà.

Tovo had sung the whole cycle of the *Lays* for him, all those songs that had never once been translated into Shaian, the lists of islands and stars, of plants and families, of the creatures of Ani and the mysteries of Vou'a.

And so Kip had gone west in a Shaian ship and returned from the east in a boat of his own hands' building, and at the Gates of the Sea he had found Ani's Tear.

Kip finished his story with the traditional words, stumbling over them a little when they came out in Shaian rather than Islander. Tovo closed his eyes, fixing in his mind this incredible story, the *inconceivable* fact he had never heard a whisper of it before.

Finally he opened his eyes to look hard at his great-nephew. "Never have I heard that you sailed the Wide Seas in a boat of your own hands' shaping, boy."

Kip should have boasted of it. He should have sung forth his deeds just as the Ancestors were said to have done. He knew the patterns: they were there in the *Lays*, the way the great sailors of the past had found new islands and come home to tell the people of them.

"No, Buru," said Kip quietly, as if he were ashamed.

"And why not?"

Kip hesitated, and then said simply: "At the time no one

asked me how I had come home, and I did not choose to speak of it later."

Kip's friends, the stars of his life, did not understand his reticence either. That meant it was not a velioi custom at all, rather a quirk of Kip's mind.

Tovo remembered again that hesitant attempt to talk to him, when Tovo had brushed him off, assuming Kip would come to him if it were important.

No one could cross the Wide Seas alone and remain unchanged: that was in every story of the sea the Islanders had.

Kip's hand went to his efela ko, curling around the central obsidian pendant with a habitual gesture.

"Efela ko," Tovo said. "And to you?"

"All that I am is held in my beginning," Kip said, describing the pearls and obsidian. The sunrise was deep in his eyes; probably deeper than he himself could feel. Some emotions were like that.

Tovo could not resist, and reached for the efani. Ani's Tear, heavy and glossy, beautiful as the sea. In the *Lays* it was only ever given to mark someone who *held the sea*.

("No one could hold the sea," Kip had complained, as every apprentice complained.

"Not many efani to be found, that's for certain," Tovo had replied equably.

Not many efani; and hardly any efevoa, either, and yet Kip held both.)

He glanced across at Kip's emperor, the sun of his life, who was looking on Kip as if he were the stone upon which the world turned.

Tovo remembered meeting this man's uncle, the emperor he himself had gone to see, and how wanting that man had been. It was a gift to see two such friends, fulfilling the ancient pattern of the *Lays*, who should be thus named in the *Lays* as having done so.

"It is the crescent moon four days from now. The Fisherman stands in the sky," Tovo said. That was largely a function of latitude—he pretty well always stood upright at the equator—but that didn't matter, not for the rightness of the moment. "You will dance Aōteketētana then before your community here."

Not that Tovo needed to see it, after that story. But Kip needed to show him.

5

I n the days after the fire dance Tovo spoke often with Kip and Vinyë's son Gaudy, and also with those of Kip's friends who came to visit him.

The most interesting, in many ways, was Kip's emperor.

One day he came to see Tovo while Kip was busy with some meeting. Tovo had gone for a walk in the gardens, looking at the tui tree and thinking that it would soon be time to return home. He had found what he had come to find—found more than that, even. Found not just a Kip who had not forgotten all the old ways for his velioi life but a Kip who had taken the *Lays* and made them the very canoe on which he sailed.

All he needed to be tana-tai was the striking stone, the tanaea. But he did not ask Tovo, and so though the words were there behind his teeth, Tovo kept them behind his teeth. Kip had learned much since those days when he refused ever to stop, but he still needed to learn when it was time to ask the questions.

One day. One day Kip would come home, when he had found his answers and learned his questions. And probably when he had gained or been given a striking-stone in some strange fashion too, for Kip had worked hard to enter the *Lays* and he had not left them yet.

One day.

In the meantime: Kip's emperor had odd eyes.

Tovo had come back from the gardens and was in Kip's sitting room, looking at the efela in their basket, admiring again the colours of Ani's Tear and the long strand of efevoa. He had spent a few minutes admiring the painting as well, thinking that he had been more handsome in his youth than he remembered.

The emperor came into the room without fanfare, nodding at his guards to stay back. Tovo turned without much surprise—the man had come when Kip was sure to be away, which meant he had come to see Tovo—-and greeted him with respect, but no more respect than he'd show any great chief. He was the tanà, the tana-tai; he was no chief nor paramount chief, but when he spoke five generations of chiefs listened.

Kip's emperor looked from Tovo to the painting and said, in a quiet, courteous voice, "May I ask you, Tanà Tovo, how that painting came to be painted?"

Tovo looked at those strange golden eyes, almost the colour of the sundrop cowries, the efevoa. They had power in them, and vision, strength; and sorrow, and hard-learned patience. Tovo did not think this man was any more patient by nature than Kip was. Or than he himself had been, for that matter.

He nodded shortly. "Suppose so. You like to sit, I suppose."

Kip's emperor nodded and chose one of the seats. His clothes rustled around him, puffing soft perfumes. Tovo sat down across from him, sinking back into the couch. His feet didn't quite touch the ground when he sat all the way back.

He tucked his feet up under him, and tilted his head at the painting.

"Do you want the short or long version?"

"Whichever is the one you think I should hear."

A good answer, Tovo thought, nodding. Somewhere in the middle, then, for Kip's great friend.

"When I was a young man, maybe twenty years old, I set out into the world. East first, then west, that's the way we go. I sailed, oh, far and far. All the way east, past the Sociables, past Nijan and Jilkano, all the way till I hit the edge of the Wide Seas. Then I turned north, following the currents north, and sailed back across to the west, all the way across until I came to the land on the other side."

"Kavanduru," Kip's emperor murmured.

"We called it *the broken edge*. The eastern edge, that's all one land, north to south. The western edge, there are bays and rivers and islands, it's all broken up. I was looking for ... perhaps you'll hear one day. I found the emperor's heir, your uncle."

"Yes."

No love lost there, Tovo heard. The man, Kip's emperor, sat there with quite possibly the most uninformative posture Tovo had ever seen. It reminded him a little of a dancer about to perform, that sense of self gathered in deep and held close. But Kip's emperor was like that all the time, never releasing his grip.

Velioi.

Tovo nodded. "All these boats. Ships, they called them." He snorted. "Didn't dare go out of sight of land. Overburdened. Much too fancy. Timid."

"The ships?" Kip's emperor asked, his voice just as uninformative as the rest of him now.

Tovo looked up into his strange efevoa-gold eyes, and saw a deep, submarine sort of amusement.

Oh, he could see why Kip had stayed.

"Someone always goes," Tovo said, not looking away. "We all want to be Elonoa'a finding an emperor worth staying for."

Oh and now there was a reaction, a stillness, a singular swallow. What a discipline!

Tovo grinned up at this man who dared not show his pleasure at being an emperor worth staying for, in the estimation of a man as great as the one that Kip had become.

"So I went. I dressed up in my festival wear, just in case," he said, gesturing at the painting, his efela and flowers, decorated for an encounter with those who might have something worth trading. "Sailed up to the fanciest boat of all of them. Elonoa'a himself couldn't have sailed it through a squall, it was so heavy with its own importance. I told the people I wanted to see this prince, and I was young then, and good-looking, and he was bored, that prince. Never met anyone so bored as he was."

Another flash through the gold eyes, but no motion, not even a swallow. Just a polite, attentive curiosity.

"He was young then, too, and good-looking, I suppose," Tovo said, and shrugged. "I was curious. I'd heard the velioi princes were ... what's the word people use? *Sophisticated*." He grinned at Kip's emperor, whose eyes were widening despite all the control and discipline.

Tovo cackled. "Aye, and he was curious about this ... what would word did he use? *Exotic? Barbarian? Savage?* Something like that. Kip wouldn't like it."

"No," Kip's emperor said, just a breath.

What fools they were, these two. The stone that hold fasts, the sun in the sky, all the grand songs of friendship and love. Tovo wondered if Kip had ever told his emperor about Elonoa'a.

Probably not.

Tovo hitched his skirt up, hooked his thumbs into the

waistband. "Not sure about *sophistication*. He liked to take, that one. Now I don't mind giving, I was tanà then as I am tanà now, and we give freely. Harder to learn to receive, for those who give by nature," he said, eyes intent on Kip's emperor's. "Maybe harder to learn to receive for those who are accustomed to taking." He snorted. "That uncle of yours knew how to take, that's sure, but not all of what was given. He was hungry but he did not know good food when he found it."

Kip's emperor stared at him, his lips twitching before he firmed them into a grave, serious, dignified sort of expression. Oh, Tovo could see why Kip had stayed for him. If he'd been forty years younger!

Seventy years younger. Tovo had met one worth standing beside on his way home, after all.

"A day or two was enough for me," Tovo said. "Tasted a few new things, *sophisticated* things, posed for the painter and her apprentice, gave a few things to that uncle of yours he *didn't* know how to take, oh, no!"

He grinned at Kip's emperor, moved his hips a little, cut his glance to the portrait, the wicked gleam the artist had found. A good artist, though her apprentice had done most of the work. He'd been better for a romp and a rumble than the emperor had been, that was for sure. *He* understood the give and the take.

"And then you sailed away again into the Wide Seas," Kip's emperor said, his voice calm, his eyes sharp as the sun on a wave.

"Wasn't going to stay for him," Tovo agreed. "Some sparks don't catch."

~

He had another conversation with Kip's emperor, the day he had decided it was about time to head home.

Kip was off again at one of his meetings. Tovo had, over the days of his visit, been both impressed and scandalized at how much time Kip spent working.

He tried to think where the man had learned it. Not from Tovo, he didn't think. Nor from most people in the Ring; this was not the Islander way, no not at all. Kip's friends seemed to feel he worked a bit too much as well, so it wasn't them, either.

Artists might spend this much time about their art, if they were very serious about it.

Tovo turned that thought over in his mind as he looked once more through Kip's basket of efela. The efani was an incredible shell, and he held it in his hands, feeling the vibrations of the distant sea, looking for where someone might attach a cord to turn it into an efela proper.

Kip's emperor came in before Tovo had much opportunity to chew over the idea. Tovo nodded at him, noting that the guards had come in again but stood by the door, faces blank.

"Must be strange, having guards with you all the time," Tovo said, nodding at the two men, who did not respond.

Kip's emperor looked at him with that breaking-wave expression in his eyes, though his body remained as neutral as before. "It is an old, old tradition for the emperors of Astandalas," he said. "Part of the job, you might say."

Not a good part, to Tovo's mind, but then he'd always been considered oddly independent, preferring to travel alone or with his apprentice. Tovo had never wanted a crowd around him, even if sometimes he wondered what it would be like to travel in one of the great double-hulled parahë like the *Lays* described, taking a crew of thirty off on adventure.

"Were you looking for me?" Tovo asked, when the man just stood there, looking at him.

"I was."

Tovo waited. He had asked the opening question; now to

look, to listen. The guards stood in their attentive, blank way. Kip's emperor stood with his shoulders back and his chin up, his eyes shadowed almost to brown. He was dressed in some shining white cloth, with a heavily embroidered gold-and-white poncho-like thing over his shoulders.

It probably wasn't called a poncho.

"I understand from Cliopher that you intend to resume your travels soon."

"That's right."

"Cliopher ... does not always ask for things he should," Kip's emperor said, quietly, a little tentatively.

"That's right," Tovo agreed.

"Would you like to travel back to the Vangavaye-ve on one of the sky ships? It would take three days, I believe."

Three days instead of three months. Tovo regarded the man before him, his fine features and his lack of emotion. Velioi. The effort it took to be that controlled really didn't seem worth it.

Obligations, now those Tovo understood. But this was not an obligation on him: this was a gift Kip's emperor was giving Kip, in a way that Kip could not refuse.

Oh, he was a clever one. Tovo would have liked to see him relax a little, let himself step into the person he was forever holding himself back from being, but you couldn't have everything.

He grinned up at the tall man. "Could be fun, flying."

The ship was in the velioi style, with a deep rounded hull and three ranks of masts. The sails were canvas, maybe, some sort of cloth, and were a fine striped white and yellow.

The captain was a wontok, Diogen from the Sociable Isles, and so were several of his crew. They were pleased to have

Tovo on board; from their comments Tovo gathered they felt a fierce partiality for Kip, as they were usually the ship he took to go home, and felt he was theirs.

Not bad, not bad.

The captain had a parrot he called Kip. It cried any number of obscenities in Quintus's voice, and *My Lord!* in what was, honestly, a pretty good approximation of Kip's.

Diogen was embarrassed, but when he saw that Tovo just laughed, he explained how he and Quintus had gone out drinking one night, and met a man named Achillon, who had ferried Kip and his emperor across to Lesuia on their holiday. Achillon had been given a parrot that Kip's emperor had enchanted somehow, but his wife had turned to be allergic so he was trying to persuade Quintus to buy it.

Quintus had happily taught it obscenities but it was Diogen the parrot had decided to adopt, which had caused him a few pangs of apprehension when he realized that the human Kip would likely travel with him in future.

Tovo thought Kip would probably find the parrot as funny as he himself did, but he also thought it did Diogen some good to have such a minor problem to worry over. Sometimes it was important to have that sort of distraction.

He'd have to say something to Quintus, too. Kip wasn't the only one who needed to be shaken up from time to time.

The view over the grey mountains was interesting. It was odd but beautiful to see the Wide Seas from above. They sailed over a handful of islands Tovo had visited in the past, and he looked down on the great lagoon of Lusoaraka with interest.

But it was the Vangavaye-ve when they reached it that made him wonder at the ingenuity of human achievement and the beauty of the world around him.

It was nearing sunrise when Diogen came to knock on his door and wake him so he could witness the Ring come into view over the western horizon.

Tovo had found the cabin nearly as fancy as Kip's rooms, if a bit smaller, and was glad for the poncho—the air was cold, this high above the surface of the sea. He ambled out to stand at the look-out in the prow, next to the sailor on watch.

It took Tovo a few minutes to relate what he was seeing to his knowledge of the Ring, but those were *his* islands, high and low, islets and reefs, and the sailor had only to point out the high peak of Linaroa for the rest to come into proper relation.

What a gift to the god of mystery, Tovo thought, watching the ordinary magic of dawn cast an extraordinary light across the sea, the Ring, the Bay of the Waters. The eastern islands' shadows were a deep blue, and then the centre of the bay gleamed silvery.

Tovo had no idea how the ship ascended and descended. Diogen had said something about the sails and some sort of ballast and something to do with the keel, but it was all velioi terms and Tovo did not feel the need to learn how this ship flew.

He stood there, balanced as the ship tilted and spiralled down, one hand on a railing the watch-sailor had insisted he hold onto. Tovo felt no fear of falling, of unbalancing, but he held the railing in obedience to the woman's concern. She called him *grandfather*, polite as polite could be.

There was Pau'lo'en'lai, the folded jungle where no one living walked. There were the cries of the seabirds, thin and high with the distance, as if Tovo heard them far out at sea. There was the brilliant spread of Gorjo City in two crescents around the volcanic islands of Mama Ituri and her Son, green and black for the peaks, all bright colours of buildings and turquoise lagoons for the city.

He took a deep breath. His nose wasn't so good as it used to be, but he could smell the flowers of home. It was odd for they were night-flowers, their scents usually disappeared by this time of the morning. Slowly rising up from the land, he guessed, blooming invisibly in the air above the Ring.

The captain brought the ship to a smooth halt at the top of the Spire, which was a feat of sailing Tovo applauded. He thanked Diogen and the sailors for their efforts, tapped Kip the Parrot on the beak, danced back before the bird took off his finger, and with his bag over his shoulder he pattered down the tight spiral stair.

At the base he discovered that Kip had sent a letter ahead, for Lazo was waiting there for him.

Tovo grinned at him as he stopped to catch his breath and look out at the familiar Ring.

"You've been on quite the journey," Lazo said, taking the poncho from Tovo after he pulled it over his head.

"Thought it about time I visited Kip," Tovo agreed.

Lazo paused a moment, but unlike Kip he had long since learned to ask questions. "And what did you find?"

Tovo looked out at the city, the waters shimmering in the sunrise-light peeking through the passes between the eastern islands, the cries of the birds and the scent of daytime flowers starting to unfurl.

"It's about time to go diving for a fine piece of fire coral," he said at last, fingering his own efetana.

Lazo made a strange, strangled exclamation.

Tovo grinned at him. "Someone always goes," he said complacently. "Kip'll come home when it's time."

AUTHOR'S NOTE

Portrait of a Wide Seas Islander is a companion story to *The Hands of the Emperor*. Other stories in *Lays of the Hearth-Fire* include the novella *Petty Treasons;* the sequel to *Hands of the Emperor, At the Feet of the Sun*, is expected later in 2022.

For further information and to stay in touch, please visit www.victoriagoddard.ca.

www.ingramcontent.com/pod-product-compliance
Lightning Source LLC
Chambersburg PA
CBHW020344220726
48290CB00013B/945